# THE LAST LETTER
## A NOVEL

# THE LAST LETTER
## A NOVEL

Susan Pogorzelski

BROWN
BEAGLE
BOOKS

*Pennsylvania*

Brown Beagle Books, Lititz, PA
www.brownbeaglebooks.com

ISBN Paperback: 978-0-9888751-3-5
ISBN Digital: 978-0-9888751-4-2
LCCN: 2016912307

Cover Design by Andrew Brown, designforwriters.com
Interior Design by Rebecca Brown, designforwriters.com

Visit the author's website at www.susanpogorzelski.com

Printed in the United States of America

FOR MY FAMILY,
*you are my lifeline.*

FOR MY FRIENDS,
*you are my strength.*

FOR MY DOCTORS,
*you are my hope.*

FOR MY FELLOW LYME WARRIORS,
*you are my heroes.*

AND FOR YOU, WHOEVER YOU ARE,
*I hope you always remember that you never walk alone.*

PART ONE

Dear Whoever You Are,

I'm not writing this letter because I want to. I'm writing because he asked me to in a way that didn't seem like a suggestion, if you know what I mean. When I told him about my time capsule, he leaned forward like he was actually curious about what I had to say for the first time since I stepped foot in his office.

"What kind of time capsule?" he asked, pen poised in his hand.

The kind you stick in the ground and wait a million gazillion years for the last surviving members of our species to dig up while excavating a barren landscape looking for traces of our humanity. The kind that looks like a My Little Pony lunchbox that you save from another of your mom's "let's throw your childhood away" garage sales in case you move someplace exotic like Norway or Iceland or South Dakota. The kind that preserves your very existence, buried and forgotten approximately two feet beneath the soil in a small corner of your dad's flower garden with only a statue of a turtle marking its memorial.

You know. That kind of time capsule.

"Just a box," I said.

"And you said you write letters?" He glanced down at

his yellow legal pad, even though he was echoing what I'd said barely three minutes earlier. "Letters to who?"

"Does it matter?"

I didn't want to be defiant. I promise, I wasn't trying to be. I just wanted to know if it mattered—if any of this did. You matter to me. You, whoever you are that's reading this now. You matter to me. Isn't that enough?

He paused and folded his arms across his desk, making the papers beneath his elbows crinkle and crease. My gaze shifted from the writing pad to the manila folder with my name scribbled in permanent marker across the tab. Anything he wrote on those pages would be stuffed in that folder and filed in the back of a cabinet somewhere, forgotten until my next appointment. I knew that. I knew this was just his job—that he would have patients before me and after me in a cycle of scheduled hours that turned into days, and those days would become weeks, and those weeks would become a lifetime of stories that no one else would ever hear.

Just because he had a kind face and a nice office and one wall at the far end of the room completely filled with degrees and certificates to prove his ability to do what he did, it didn't mean he cared to know me. Not really know me, anyway. He was exactly like my guidance counselor who called me into his office because I got a "D" on my history test—I was just another problem to solve, with one bad grade leading me there.

"But it wasn't just one bad grade, was it?"

No. But that's why I was there today, sitting in his nice office with all those bookcases and staring at a bunch of weird sculpture-things on his desk that looked more like toys than anything else and seemed to serve no purpose at all.

That's why I'm here now, writing you this letter.

"Is that really the only reason you're here?" he asked, eyebrows raised.

No, but he already knew that.

We stared at each other, the silence lingering between us like a tornado gathering strength, accumulating all the words that would remain unspoken, until he leaned back in his leather chair and tilted his head and said, "What makes you afraid?" in this tone of voice that made it seem like he already knew the answer, he just wanted to hear it from me.

I wanted to tell him I wasn't afraid of anything—that we were there to talk about how Dr. Denlinger couldn't find anything wrong with me physically, so could we please go back to figuring out why I'm having trouble sleeping at night and why that's causing me to become stupid in school instead of talking about whatever it was he was trying to get me to talk about?

"What do you think, Amelia?"

I think sometimes insomnia is just insomnia, especially when you're fifteen years old. But he didn't want to hear that. Because it couldn't be that simple.

So I told him what he wanted to hear—that the world's going to end soon and Earth will cease to exist. At least, that's what all the doomsday prophecies and the preacher shouting at cars off the exit ramp of I-81 every Monday and Thursday morning seem to think. They keep calling it Y2K, even though that's just a fancy way of saying it's the new millennium, but it's supposed to be a global disaster where every computer in the world shuts down because it doesn't recognize the date, and *that* will cause all the power generators to explode and the world to go dark or something crazy like that.

If that wasn't enough, the preacher keeps yelling about an asteroid headed our way that can take out the earth like the one that took out the dinosaurs, and apparently NASA is holding their breath and recalculating the trajectory every .5 seconds. According to the preacher, it's preordained. According to Mr. Vick, my astronomy teacher, asteroids are flying by us at a thousand miles per hour every single second.

So it's either this whole Y2K business or an Earth-destroying asteroid that'll knock us out, but nobody knows for sure and there's no real proof of anything. In the meantime, people are buying cases of bottled water and canned carrots in bulk and hoarding sleeping bags and generators in their basements.

Because if an asteroid is going to annihilate the earth, hiding in the ground is exactly where I want to be.

"Is that what you're afraid of?" he asked, his tone surprisingly absent of any judgment. "That the earth is going to be annihilated?"

No.

I was just saying it's a strong possibility. And believe me, I should know—thanks to my mom, I learned all about the destruction of Pompeii and Herculaneum before I knew Mister Rogers even had a neighborhood.

"Your mom… Her name's Karen?"

I nodded. "You can meet her, if you want. She's out in the waiting room."

He leaned back in his chair. "Why don't you tell me about her."

She's a history professor at the local community college where my older brother's a freshman. Her students love her because she's always going off on tangents about some disaster or another and humanity's ability to endure like it's some kind of story time for adults. My mom talks about tragedies with a sigh in her voice and hope in her eyes. She says people just want to be prepared, that they want a guarantee of survival. I don't think there is any guarantee of survival—it seems to me surviving is nothing more than a roll of the dice.

"But your mom doesn't believe that," he confirmed.

"No," I said. "I don't think so."

Then again, that's probably why she named me and my brother and sister after survivors of famous historical tragedies. Not many people know that. It's not a secret or anything, I just don't think anyone would understand it. I used to be embarrassed by my name, but she always said it was something to be proud of—that names are significant and they help form a person's identity—and when you hear something an infinite number of times, you begin to believe it.

"It's a bit unusual," he agreed, glancing at the file on his desk.

I get that they're her heroes—Amelia Garrett because she survived the sinking of the Titanic, and Samuel Breck because he survived the outbreak of Yellow Fever in Philadelphia, and Isabella Breen because she survived trekking across the United States with a group of pioneers who apparently resorted to cannibalism when the winter got really bad. I get it. Everyone needs a hero. But it seems a little backwards, doesn't it? When you think about it, shouldn't we be named after the people who actually died instead of the ones that didn't? Like an "in memoriam" kind of thing? I mean, it's a valid question, isn't it?

But when I asked my mom this once, she just paused and looked at me blankly and said, "Don't be morbid, Lia."

Because clearly I'm the one who's morbid.

So here we all are—or here we all *were*. My brother and sister and me. Living epitaphs, proof of survival of the fittest. Or maybe our namesakes just got lucky.

If you're actually reading this, maybe this Y2K thing never happened and the earth wasn't completely obliterated by an asteroid. Maybe life still goes on and on and on.

Maybe I got lucky, too.

"What do you write in these letters?" he tried again.

Nothing. Everything. Too much and not enough.

"I don't know," I said. It was as close to the truth as I could get. Because I do know—and I don't. And even if I could formulate an answer that would make sense to someone like him, I don't think I would say anything even then.

This is mine and mine alone—something the world can't take from me. I know what he was trying to do—it's what everyone tries to do. They try to shape you and mold you and classify you, try to create some kind of identity for you based on fragments of who they think you are. I'm only fifteen—I'm not even sure I have an identity yet, but isn't that for me to decide?

Maybe that's why I'm writing to you, did anyone ever think of that? You don't know who I am—and I don't know who I am—and so this is a place where I can figure that out, not by talking to some doctor who pretends to want to know me, but by saying what I want to say and feeling what I want to feel. I can be myself and ask the questions I need to ask and change my mind and second-guess myself, and no one would care.

Because you're the only one who will ever read this when you find this.

If you find this.

He sighed, his dark blue eyes flicking over my shoulder to the digital clock displayed on one of the bookshelves against the back wall with numbers so large, it was the first thing I noticed when I walked in.

"Do me a favor," he began. For the first time in an hour, I heard something in his voice that made him seem—I don't know, *human*. "Write one more letter tonight. Everything you couldn't tell me—put it to the page and seal it up in your time capsule. Just make sure you say the words. Okay?"

I nodded slowly, suddenly sad and regretting that we had spent the whole hour talking and neither of us had said anything. Because, like it or not, here was someone who knew my story now—at least, the beginning of it. And even though I haven't figured out who I am yet, I'm still here—Amelia Garrett Lenelli—I'm still someone, and he's someone who knows that, who knows I exist. When your whole world is about to be destroyed by a blackout or an asteroid, maybe that's enough.

He ripped his notes free from the legal pad and tucked the stray pages into the manila file folder. I stood and bunched my winter coat in my arms, hesitating in front of his desk.

"We didn't talk about my insomnia—about what happened," I said.

He smiled a nice, warm smile, and I swear there was a hint of amusement layered within his next words. "We'll talk next week."

I couldn't help but smile back. "I like that you're an optimist."

Anyone can dig up my dad's garden. Anyone can find my old lunchbox and read these letters, but who actually will? They won't mean anything unless you want them to. Right now, I'm just one more anonymous person in a sea of millions.

Except I'm not anonymous if you're reading this, am I? Because even if I don't know you—even if I'll never know you—now you know me. You know my name. You know my story.

I only exist if you choose to see me.

So I guess that's the real question.

Do you see me?

**JANUARY 4, 2000**

Dear Whoever You Are,

The real tragedy in life is that time moves too slowly, and yet there never seems to be enough of it. We can spend the majority of our days anticipating the big something while the little nothings tick by, second by second, and before we know it, whole lifetimes have passed and we've just been *wait-ing, wait-ing, wait-ing* for the next heartbeat of an internal clock to tell us that life can't be only this.

"How are you sleeping?" he greeted me in the open door-way to his office.

That was it. No, "How are you, Happy New Year, glad you survived the apocalypse." Just, "How are you sleeping," like everything would be different now and my insomnia would be magically cured.

I walked past him into his office and glanced at the uncomfortable wooden chair across from his desk, then dropped my coat on the paisley couch near the windows and plopped down next to it. He paused halfway to his desk, opened his mouth like he wanted to say something, then decided against it, turned one of the wooden chairs around to face me, and reached for his notepad and pen instead.

"Do you feel relieved?" he asked.

"Relieved at what?"

"That we've entered a new millennium..."

Now that the asteroid has passed by Earth without blow-ing us up—that's what he meant. Now that the world's computers didn't freak out and cause the whole world to go dark. I don't know why anyone thought anything would be different in the first place. It's like we wait for these disas-ters—we plan for them and anticipate them like we *want* them to happen because it means something exciting will break up the momentum that is our daily, average, everyday existence. And then, when nothing happens—when the earth isn't obliterated by an object hurtling at us from space at a million miles an hour—we're disappointed.

And I'm the one seeing a shrink.

"I think it's just another year of a brand-new century," I said. "Today is just another day."

I wonder what everyone in their shelters are thinking—if they're climbing out of their bunkers, blinking against the brightness of the sun, wondering what's different in the world. I wonder if they're disappointed to see that nothing has changed.

Not one thing.

It makes me sad.

"Sad?" he repeated.

"Just a little…"

It's just that we're all like them—those doomsdayers in their bunkers. Every single one of us. We're all spending our lives in the darkness of some shelter waiting for something big to happen, when life is really just a series of moments that we hope one day adds up to something more. I want my life to be something more. Is that selfish? To want something more than what you have when what you have is already more than enough? I can't help but want more—like I expect more.

"Have you always lived here?" I asked him.

He looked surprised by the question, like maybe he didn't expect me to ask him about himself, like maybe he preferred it that way. "I grew up here—over on Applewood, near the church."

I sat up. "That's my neighborhood—the street with the dead-end drive."

He chuckled like I'd said something funny, then set the notepad on the desk and reached for his yellow coffee mug instead. "That leads to the woods… That's the one."

"Which house is yours?"

"It was my dad's house. He left it to me after my mom died, after—" A shadow crossed his face, but he cleared his throat, tossing aside the memory. "Anyway—large porch, green shutters, two chimneys. There was a crab apple tree in the side yard."

"Do you still live there?"

"Nah. I left for a while—sold the house and did some traveling, met my wife in New York, went to school, had my kids, came back here to see if anything had changed."

"And had it?"

He paused. "I'd changed. That was enough."

I want to travel the world. I want to play with the elephants in Thailand and go on a safari to see the gorillas in Uganda and visit the ruins of Machu Picchu in Peru. But how likely is that? I mean, those are just dreams, right? They're dreams everyone has, and how many people actually go out and do it?

How would I do it, anyway? I'm still in high school. It'll be years and years and years before any of it is even possible, and who knows if that will still be my dream then. Who knows if we'll even be here, if there won't be some other global disaster for the preacher to shout about and we'll go the way of the ancient Incas after all—here one day, gone the next.

"I don't think I'd ever come back if I left," I said.

"You'd be surprised." He rolled the coffee mug in his hands, glancing at the contents that had grown cold within. "Sometimes the same song can sound different depending on where you've been."

Maybe that's what this is. Maybe by the time you find these letters, they'll be a relic—a reminder of another lost civilization that you keep under lock and key in a museum somewhere, waiting to be curated. Maybe these letters are important because they tell you who we were and how we lived. Maybe I have dreams just like the ancient Incas did. Maybe you have dreams like I do. Maybe nothing is so different—that we're not so different—after all.

"Did you write your letter?" I nodded. "And how did that go?"

"The ground's frozen," I said. "I won't be able to add it to my time capsule until May."

"That's okay." He set the mug on his desk, the ceramic meeting the wood in a hollow greeting. "Tell me how you're feeling now that the asteroid's gone. Still afraid?"

"I was never afraid of the asteroid," I said.

"So, what were you afraid of?"

Or maybe it's nothing. Maybe this time capsule is forgotten again—simply stuffed in a crate with old maps and family trees and abandoned under the attic eaves.

"Amelia?"

Maybe you dig this up without even bothering to look inside—a cheap, plastic My Little Pony lunchbox that's tossed in the garbage and hauled away on Thursday mornings.

Nothing to keep. Nothing to lose.

Nothing at all.

*~ Amelia*

FEBRUARY 3, 2000

Dear Whoever You Are,

It was an Iowa rain. At least, that's what my dad called it when we drove out west to visit my grandparents on their farm last summer. It stopped as quickly as it came, leaving behind tiny pools of water that collected in the driveway and reflected off the porchlight in a layered sheen of yellow light. Thick raindrops clung to the rain gutters above the screened-in porch where my best friend, Mollie, and I lounged on cots, my little sister drawing in her sketchpad on the air mattress beside us. We pulled our blankets over our legs and turned up the volume on our Discmans and then, when even the fireflies stopped glowing, we whispered how this new year at school would be the start of everything.

Except it hasn't been much of anything.

Nothing's different from last year. That's what doesn't make sense. Nothing's different, except we're a year older, but it's not the same, either. Everything seems to be changing in this subtle, secret way I can't name, and I know, one day, I'll look back and see this giant transformation because that's what change really looks like. Change is big and scary and you always see it coming—like the flickering lights of a worldwide blackout or an asteroid smacking into the earth. That's what change is supposed to be. But this...

Right now, I can only catch a glimpse of something, and I don't know what it's supposed to be or where it's leading—

Or how to stop it.

That's what I felt those first few weeks of high school this year. The change in pressure, the rumblings in the atmosphere, the feeling that something was happening underneath the surface with every note passed in study hall or whisper of gossip at lunch or the first, disapproving frown from my history teacher when she realized Sam was my brother.

It hasn't been what I imagined it to be—maybe that's my problem. It's not what we planned for all summer long, not what we whispered about on my grandparents' porch in Iowa.

The sky had darkened quickly. Heavy raindrops splattered on the roof, one after the next in an undefined rhythm until it became a rush of rain, drowning out the laugh tracks from the TV inside. My dad stepped onto the porch, hands in his pockets, and leaned against the pillar, his eyes trained on the fields where cornstalks were just beginning to grow tall.

"Think there'll be a tornado?" Mollie asked him.

Izzy whipped her head around, her eyes wide. "There's gonna be a tornado?"

But Dad shook his head. "Nah. It's just a little Iowa rain. The storm will be here and gone before you know it."

I wish I could say the same about school.

It was my first "D" on a history test. It was my first "D" on anything. That was my name in the top corner of the page, and that was my handwriting. I'd circled all the wrong answers, but I knew all the right ones. Even now, I can't figure out what happened. I mean, my mom's a *history professor*. I knew more about the Byzantine Empire when I was in diapers than I knew about Big Bird.

But when I tried telling this to Mrs. Hadley after class, she just studied me over the rim of her glasses, her frown set like a permanent fixture on her face. Then she shook her head like she expected more out of me because I was Sam's sister, and maybe she didn't expect enough out of him.

Mollie had to stay after school to work on an art project, so I asked her older brother if he could drive me to see my mom at the college. I don't know—maybe I needed some kind of validation from someone who actually knew me, who knew what I knew. Or maybe I thought she would have an answer for why I suddenly became stupid during third-period history that day.

Either way, I really needed my mom.

It's strange to see your parents at work. They talk about it over dinner in the "how was your day" kind of way, and you nod and listen like you know what they're talking about. But you don't know what they're talking about because who they are at work is so far removed from everything you know about them at home. There they are, in another part of town, living a second life that's completely separate from your own—a life you know nothing about and can't begin to imagine. It's like when you're five and afraid to go to sleep at night because you believe the whole world will disappear once you close your eyes, or the way your dog has no concept of what lies beyond the neighborhood where you walk—you wonder if maybe that's the end of the world, if maybe it ceases to exist without you.

It doesn't. Of course it doesn't. But you don't know that when you're six years old and sick with a summer flu. All you know is they're not there with you, and you don't understand why. And that's the only thing that seems to matter until they pick you up from camp and help you make a bed out of two cushioned chairs in their office so you can sleep while they teach their class. Worlds collide, and suddenly they become something more, something whole—like lightning and thunder joining to create a perfect storm of someone new.

When we rounded the corner outside her office, my mom glanced at me over her student's shoulder and paused, a silent question in her eyes. Maybe it was because Josh was there, or maybe it was the death-grip I had on the paper in my hands, but she raised her eyebrow and held up her hand, and I nodded and walked further down the hallway, my heart beating like thunder in my ears, waiting for the storm to erupt.

I told Josh he didn't need to stay, that my mom could take me home when she was done with her office hours, but he shrugged and said he didn't mind and snatched the test from my hands before I could stop him. He didn't say anything as he skimmed the page. Not one single thing. I wish he had said something—it would have been a million times better if he had said something, said anything.

My heart sank, unwilling tears pricking at the corners of my eyes, knowing maybe he'd expected more out of me and, somehow, I'd failed even him. All I wanted to do was make him see me the way I was before he took that paper from my hands—as someone smart and capable and worth so much more than one bad grade. Because here was someone who'd known me my whole life, too, and now, seeing that "D" on my history test, maybe he was starting to wonder if he really knew me at all.

He stared at the paper for a long moment. Then he handed it back to me without a word and walked away to read a flyer pinned to one of the bulletin boards across the hall.

Nothing anyone said now could ever compare to that silence.

I remember how quickly the rain in Iowa passed. Just like my dad said, it came and went in a matter of minutes, flashes of lightning already fading into the horizon by the time the next commercial break came on the TV inside. But the cows in the far pasture were huddled under a small grove of trees, and the leaves on the cornstalks hung limp, weighed down by thick raindrops.

Traces of the storm always remain.

~Amelia

MARCH 7, 2000

Dear Whoever You Are,

He was sitting behind his desk again, and I was back in that uncomfortable wooden chair that groans whenever my foot goes numb and I try to shake it awake. As soon as I saw the couch in his office, I wanted to fold myself into the cushions and go to sleep. I told him we didn't have to talk—I could just crash there for the hour and we could pretend we made some progress today—but even though I was only half-joking, he frowned instead of laughed and pointed to the armchair across from him.

"Let's talk about what happened," he said, glancing at

the open file where the torn yellow sheets from his notepad were beginning to pile up.

I already told you what happened in my last letter.

"Let's talk about what really happened," he tried again.

I'm starting to not like him again, despite his nice face and the degrees hanging on his walls and the dozens of conversations we've had where he actually seems like a normal human being.

Why do doctors do that, anyway? Why do they hang their degrees on their office walls? When I graduate from college and go wherever I go to get whatever job I get, do I get to hang my degrees on the walls, too? None of my teachers are showing off their degrees, though, technically, they have a classroom, not an office. But still—they went to school, they earned it. So did my neighbor, who works as a store clerk at the mall, and Mollie's mom, who's a teller at the credit union over on Hastings Road. They're smart—shouldn't they be able to prove it to the world, too?

"They should," he agreed. "But we're not talking about my degrees today."

"You remind me of my guidance counselor now," I said.

My guidance counselor, Mr. Corrigan—who barely looked up when I stepped in the doorway of his office last fall. His computer was shoved into a corner on his desk, thick books wedged beside the monitor, the spines hidden from view. On the floor, stacks of files surrounded his chair like they'd been strategically placed according to some logic only he knew and I'm pretty sure I never want to find out.

He motioned to the empty chair beside my parents with a flick of his wrist and kept talking about the types of help available to kids like me, whatever that was supposed to mean. I slid my backpack from my shoulder and plopped into the seat, raising my eyebrows at my dad, who met my glance with a subtle wink before nodding along to whatever Mr. Corrigan was saying.

This meeting wasn't coming as some kind of a surprise to them. I'd already told them I'd failed two more tests during dinner the night before—and it wasn't for lack of trying. They knew that. So when Mr. Corrigan finally turned to me and introduced himself and asked me if I knew why we were all gathered there today, like we were his congregation and he was setting a trap for confession, I told him yes. I told him why. I told him I knew the material, but for some reason, I'd mixed up my answers, and if I knew how that happened, maybe we wouldn't be there in his office. Maybe I'd still be just a name to him, just another body in a sea of students passing in the hallways—there one year and replaced the next.

Mr. Corrigan leaned back in his chair, nodded his head like he'd heard all this before, and suggested to my parents that the pressures of high school might be too much for some students.

I almost laughed at him. I'm not that student.

Even my mom and dad traded glances. At least they knew me better than that, too.

When I tried to explain that I hadn't been sleeping well—that my mind felt like some kind of sludge I had to trudge through from the moment I opened my eyes in the morning—he glanced at my file and said I was getting an "A" in English, so it couldn't be that bad.

"I remind you of your guidance counselor?" my doctor repeated, his nose wrinkled like he didn't know whether to take it as a compliment or an insult.

"He didn't care about what I had to say, either."

He sighed, capped his pen and set it aside, and folded his hands across his desk. "I care about what you have to say, Lia."

I know. I know he did. And I immediately hated myself for saying something so mean when I know he was trying to be nice and do his job. I just don't know why we've spent an hour a week for the past six months talking about my time capsule and test grades and the end of the world that didn't happen when the reason Dr. Denlinger sent me there in the first place was because I was having trouble sleeping.

"Let's talk about what happened," he tried again.

Let's not.

*~ Amelia*

**MAY 20, 2000**

Dear Whoever You Are,

A word of advice: if you have something you love, hold onto it. Don't let anyone take it or throw it away or sell it at a garage sale for twenty-five cents because if you love it, it's worth so much more than a single quarter. If you love something, that something becomes invaluable.

It's weird how we can become so attached to things, isn't it? Like a favorite, oversized sweater you can't wait to put on as soon as the trees start to change color, even though the hem has begun to unravel because your dog chewed on it when he was a puppy. Or a blue plastic barrette you wore in your hair every single day in elementary school, and even though you wouldn't be caught dead wearing it now, there's still something about the curve and snap of the clasp that you love.

I have a pair of blue and yellow roller skates I got for my eighth birthday, when Mollie and I skated in circles on her driveway, belting out "Tomorrow" from *Annie* until her mom came outside and asked us to please, for the love of God, sing something else. There's the bin of mixed tapes recorded from the radio—perfectly timed to the exact moment when the DJ stops talking and the first lyrics start—and a collection of teen magazines from when my Grandma Lenelli bought me a subscription, with half the pages ripped out because the celebrity posters are still taped to the wall above my bed.

It's like these things become infused with memories, and every time you see them or touch them, they become so much more than objects. And you're not just being sentimental or nostalgic, either. You know these things are an extension of you—by wearing that sweater and listening to those tapes and putting up those posters, you're announcing to the world who you were and how you've become who you are.

Aren't we all trying to do that, anyway? Like my doctor and his college degrees hanging on his office walls, or Sam and his Camry that he washes every Saturday in the summer, or my dad and his collection of *The Lord of the Rings* memorabilia... Aren't we all just trying to tell the world that we're here, that we exist beyond our name? That we have interests and feelings and memories? We're the sum of all our parts, and even objects become a part of that.

Maybe that's why, when I heard the familiar sound of plastic tires grinding against the pavement this morning, it woke me up—like it woke up a memory—and I leaned across the bed and pulled aside the curtain and watched as some little kid peddled her way down the sidewalk, away from the garage sale that looked like our childhood threw up all over our lawn, and out of my life forever.

We'd set up card tables along the edge of the driveway last night and laid a tarp on the grass for the clothes we've outgrown, but with our stuff spread out like that—a lamp that had been in Mom and Dad's bedroom for years, vinyl records from Sammy's collection, Tupperware that I remember beating the hell out of when Izzy and I decided to start our own band when she was four and I was nine—it was like they were selling off pieces of us one stupid, rusted toaster at a time.

I wanted to cry.

And then, I got pissed off. I quickly dressed and flew down the stairs and ran out the door, asking my mom how she could just sell our stuff like that, like these things didn't matter, like they hadn't been in our home for the past fifteen years. She handed a customer some change, then said in a lowered voice that I'd known for weeks that she and Dad were cleaning out the basement—that if I wanted to keep something, I could have said something.

But my bike...

That little girl was already halfway down the block by now, her father walking beside her. I don't remember the first time I rode that bike—a tricycle, really, with a purple seat that lifted up so I could hide things in it like rocks and worms—but I'm pretty sure my dad was beside me when I did.

It's funny how you don't know how much you want to keep something until it's already gone.

My mom was busy folding a bunch of Sam's t-shirts, and I don't know if she heard it in my voice or saw it in my eyes, but she reached up and tried to brush my hair out of my face. I shrugged away from her.

I was angry. But the thing is, I wasn't really angry at her. I was angry at the whole stupid idea that other people could park in the street and walk on your driveway and claim something that was yours with just a dime. My mom was selling our memories like a ten cent—

She yelled at me then. Told me to watch my language and either help or go inside, and so I plopped down on the front step, stuck my chin in my hands, and watched strangers walk away with pieces of our past.

I'm glad I took the lunchbox from the basement last summer, glad it's buried now under that stupid turtle statue in the backyard so I can add this letter to it when it gets a little warmer and the ground thaws. Otherwise, my mom probably would have sold that, too.

Don't sell these letters, okay? Throw them out or burn them, or better yet, shred them so the paper can become something cool like compost or tires for a bike or a paper-maché statue, but don't sell them. Because they're not just another useless toaster.

Not to me, anyway.

When Josh pulled up an hour later, I'd already seen my roller skates go to my six year old neighbor ($5), my collection of magazines sold to a giggling trio of twelve year old girls ($0.10 a piece or $2 for all), and a shoebox full of my cassette tapes go, inexplicably, to a guy in his thirties wearing a Weezer t-shirt ($1 for the box). I couldn't help but smirk at that one. Boy, was he going to be surprised when he listened to my song selection.

I was sitting at the card table with the lockbox, scooted down low in a folding chair, my hands stuffed in the pockets of my army jacket. Josh parked across the street in front of my neighbor's mailbox, and I could see him pause as he glanced at the strangers milling about our driveway, considering whether or not they wanted to spend fifty cents on throw pillows. I considered whether or not to call them cheap asses out loud.

I watched him walk up the driveway. When he was within earshot, I asked him what he was doing there. He said some of the guys were getting together for a pick-up soccer game and were hoping Sam would want to play with his old team.

"You can come watch, if you want," he said.

"I'm busy. You know, helping my mom."

He winked. "I can see that."

I thought he would go right in the house and run up the stairs to wake Sam up, but instead he skimmed the stuff set out on the card tables, then walked over and picked up a faded stuffed lamb with a heart-shaped nose. He paused and turned it over, like he was studying it, and I watched him, but I couldn't tell what he was thinking.

"This yours?" he asked.

I shook my head. "Izzy's."

He nodded and set it back down, glanced over the table again, and shoved his hands in his pockets. "Later," he said.

Then he wandered through the garage and into the house.

I kept expecting him to say goodbye again when he and Sam came back outside, but he didn't even look at me. They just walked past me, walked past all of our memories, got in his car, and were gone.

I don't care what strangers buy and take away anymore. If my mom wants to sell our memories, she can. They're just objects, anyway—a stupid stuffed lamb that Isabella probably doesn't even remember now that she's growing up.

~*Amelia*

### JULY 11, 2000

Dear Whoever You Are,

"How was your Fourth of July?" he asked when I saw him today.

No, "How are you, Happy Independence Day, did you steal any wine coolers at the family picnic?" Straight to the point—I was starting to appreciate that about him.

"It was good," I said. "We walked over to the Engles' for their annual barbecue."

"That's Mollie and Josh," he confirmed without glancing at his notes. We were too far past that now. The manila file folder with my name on the tab remained closed and set aside, the pen just out of reach. Now, we were just two people having a conversation for an hour every week, two strangers slowly getting used to each other. "How was it?"

"The burgers were good."

My neighbors and their kids were already at the buffet when we got there, and we loaded our paper plates with potato salad and my mom's coleslaw and cheeseburgers that, somehow, are the best burgers I've ever tasted in my entire life. Every year, my dad helps Mr. Engle barbecue and tries to get him to spill his secret on what makes his burgers so good, and every year, Mr. Engle laughs and says it must be the charcoal grill. But my dad has a charcoal grill, so that's definitely not it.

"Did you see the fireworks at the park?" my doctor asked.

I didn't answer.

The community park out on Hastings Road sets off fireworks each year, but our neighborhood sits in a valley and is lined with trees, so all we can see is the sky lighting up with flashes of residual, patriotic color. Instead, we set our own fireworks off in the street. Mr. Engle and my dad used to do it when we were younger, but now they watch from the porch, talking about sports or work and sipping their beers directly from the bottles while Sam and Josh drag a box of fireworks out from the garage—some purchased from the tent set up in the grocery store parking lot and others they got from a road trip to North Carolina in June.

It made me nervous, watching them. I don't even know why.

Mollie rounded up her little brother, Justin, and Isabella and the rest of the kids, and we sat with them on the sidewalk a safe distance away. Every time a car turned down the street, the kids hollered and waved their arms so Sam and Josh could move out of the way, but aside from being run over by a car, I could think of a thousand and one ways all of this could go wrong. All I could picture were the spinners spinning out of control and hitting one of the kids, or Josh and Sam being in the line of fire whenever a rocket shot into the air, or rushing them to the hospital with third-degree burns when one of those colorful strobe fireworks blew up in their faces.

Some kids got to hear fairy tales at bedtime. We got to hear about the Hindenburg. Believe me, when you have a mother who likes to talk about disasters, it's easy to wonder what kind of disaster might happen next.

I thought about dragging the hose around from the side of the house, even though they had a plastic bucket filled with water nearby. I thought about taking them a fire extinguisher—or two—or grabbing the cordless phone from the kitchen so I could call 911 at a moment's notice. I thought about yelling at them to stop because I couldn't help imagining a car running over one of the Roman candles and igniting the gas tank, creating our own giant, destructible firework. But my dad hollered for Sam to light two of the spinners at once, and even though he didn't seem worried at all, the dread continued to build in the pit of my stomach.

I couldn't watch them anymore. I ran upstairs to Mollie's room and curled up on her bed with a book and her Discman and willed myself not to peek out her window to see what was going on in the street below.

"It's too bad you weren't feeling well," my doctor said, his blue eyes softening and growing dark with sympathy. They were a shade of blue I've never seen before—the kind of blue that reminded me of a night sky right before the stars come out. "I heard they were pretty great this year."

My eyes flicked to the silver picture frames that lined his desk. "You didn't take your kids?"

"No, no…" He shook his head. "They live in New York with their mom."

"You're divorced?" I don't know why that surprised me. Maybe it was because in all of those photographs, he looked happy, and I didn't want to imagine him being sad.

"Separated," he said. "Last year—after I came back here to take care of my dad. Are you feeling any better?"

I nodded. "Must have been bad coleslaw."

At some point, Mollie came upstairs to look for me, and I told her the truth about how I couldn't shake the feeling that something terrible was going to happen—that I couldn't stay and watch what felt like an inevitability. She tilted her head the way she does when she's trying to work through a math problem, but she didn't say anything. Instead, she pulled out a new CD and popped it in her stereo, the fireworks forgotten to everyone but me. An hour later, Sam called up the stairs, telling me to get my stuff so he could walk me home, but Mollie said I was sleeping over and then smiled like she used to when we kept each other's secrets.

It turned out, there weren't any explosions or fireworks or accidents, and I felt stupid for worrying for nothing. But that feeling in my gut had been so strong, stealing my breath with an unresolved warning that something could happen at any minute, and I don't know how that's possible.

"Can I ask you something?"

He raised his eyebrows in surprise, and I inwardly cringed, knowing where that surprise came from. It wasn't his fault that he usually had to pry words out of me. He was always there, patiently waiting for me to talk to him, to trust him, to tell him what he already knew but what he thought I needed to say out loud.

"Anything," he said. I swear there was the smallest amount of relief in his voice.

I leaned forward and tapped one of the sculptures on his desk, then sat back and watched the metal beads rock back and forth in endless rhythm. When I raised my eyes to look at him, he was waiting expectantly.

"People are always saying to trust your instincts," I said, "but if my instincts are screaming that something's a really bad idea and nothing happens, how do I trust that?"

He leaned back in his chair the way I've seen him do a thousand times before—or maybe just a dozen—and rubbed his hand along his jawline where the faint outline of bearded stubble was starting to grow. It wasn't the question he expected. Maybe he didn't know what to expect.

Maybe that was the point. Maybe you never know. Maybe that's when the bad things happen, and my worrying somehow prevented it. Because if you're prepared for the worst—if you can think of every scenario and all the ways something can go wrong—then by some divine intervention, it won't.

I think I like that. I think I'd rather think about all the bad things...

Even if they cancel out the good.

*~Amelia*

## JULY 15, 2000

Dear Whoever You Are,

They said today would be the hottest day on record, so after my dad got off from his morning shift at the vet clinic, we piled into the minivan, picked up Mollie and Justin from their house, and drove two hours to the beach for the afternoon.

It wasn't like the trips I remembered—like the time Sammy tried to teach me how to boogie board or when Izzy and I won a sandcastle contest near the boardwalk. We didn't splash in the water or collect broken seashells along the shoreline or race each other to the pier.

Actually, we didn't do much of anything.

The beach was too crowded—there were too many people swimming and too many seagulls trying to steal the sandwiches from our hands and too many kids screaming at the top of their lungs. But if I lay on my towel and closed my eyes, I could block it all out. My dad's low voice instructing Justin on a trick with the soccer ball became a low, comforting murmur. The sound of change clinking in my mom's purse became a melody, intertwining with her soft request to Izzy and Mollie to bring her back an orange creamsicle from the snack stand. And then, even that faded.

Because if I closed my eyes, the world around me disappeared, and I could see what I wanted to see and hear what I wanted to hear, and right then, all I wanted was to feel the heat of the sun pressing against my eyelids and listen to the endlessness of the ocean. The waves could try to reach me, but they'd never get close enough.

The sun could try to burn me, but it could never be hot enough.

I felt invincible. In that moment, I belonged to forever.

I was melting into the earth, fading from the reality that was occurring around me and becoming a part of something more profound. I belonged to each grain of sand beneath my back and the ocean that scattered mist at my feet and the sky whose breeze wrapped around me like a cocoon or a chrysalis—the one that turns you into a butterfly, not a moth.

I was young and old at exactly the same time, like I was caught in this eternal in-between where age didn't matter and time didn't exist, and if I told this to anyone else, they would think I'd smoked one of the joints I found in Sam's glove box last week. I haven't, I swear.

But you understand, don't you? You've had that feeling before, haven't you?

Maybe it was nothing. Maybe it was too much sun and not enough water. Because it lasted for only a second before Justin kicked the soccer ball and sprayed sand across my beach towel, and no matter how hard I tried later, I couldn't get that feeling back. It's just as well. I'm not even sixteen yet. I don't belong to anything more profound than my school or my neighborhood or my family.

But I can't stop wishing that I did.

I almost told this to Josh tonight. It was after dark when we dropped Mollie and Justin off at their house, and when we got home, he was playing basketball with Sam in our driveway, the light from the open garage door spilling onto the pavement. My dad parked in the street and told us we could unload the car in the morning, but he carried the cooler into the house and Mom reminded us to take in the wet towels. Izzy grabbed her beach bag while I folded the towels over my arms, and just as I was walking past them up the driveway, Josh paused and juggled the basketball in his hands and asked me if I wanted to play. I was wearing flip-flops and smelled like the beach, and all I wanted to do was take a shower so I smelled like raspberry shampoo instead.

I hesitated. I felt like I couldn't move and couldn't speak, like I was stuck in that in-between again, only now in a bad way. And he just looked at me—not impatiently or anything, just waiting. I wanted to tell him then. I thought if anyone might understand whatever that was today on the beach, it would be him. Because he's like that—he jokes around and acts all goofy with Sam, but then he'll come up with something smart and poetic to say, and it makes you want to stay up all night talking to him about feeling like life is bigger than you and how somehow you're a part of it and then missing that feeling when it's gone.

But Sam hollered for the ball, and Izzy and my dad came back outside suggesting a game of two-on-two, and instead of taking a shower, I went up to my room and lay down on my bed, shaking the sand from my shorts and hoping I had brought some of the beach back with me after all.

*~Amelia*

Dear Whoever You Are,

I feel like I know you.

Okay, so that was a stupid thing to write. I know I don't know you. I don't know who you are or where you are or when you'll be reading this, if you're even reading this at all. I'm pretty much writing to myself here, and I know that. But it helps to write it all down and say what needs to be said instead of hoarding the words when I don't want them, anyway. Because putting what I'm feeling down on paper and dispelling the thoughts from my mind is a form of relief, and if I can get rid of this pain, then maybe I can make room for something else—something better—instead.

At least, that's what my doctor said the first time I told him about my time capsule.

I know I can talk to him—there's a one-hour appointment penciled in each month on the kitchen calendar that says I have to talk to him—but it's not the same way I can talk to you. Maybe I could mention it to Mom and Dad, but they get this annoying "we were your age once, you know" flicker in their eyes, and Sammy would listen, but then he'd tell me to quit being so sensitive, and Izzy would sympathize, but she's eleven and in middle school, and when you're eleven and in middle school, you have a whole host of other problems, believe me.

Then there's Mollie—my best friend and the one person on Earth I'm supposed to be able to talk to about anything, but this has everything to do with her, so I can't.

But I can talk to you. I can tell you things I can't tell anyone else because you're the only one who'll read this—if you read this—and I like that my secrets will be bundled up in these letters, buried and forgotten like they were never there at all.

Mollie and I kept each other's secrets once—silly, stupid promises not to tell anyone how we played songs to Scott Abernathy over the phone and then hung up before he could tell it was us, or the time her dad dropped us off at the movies and we spent the money playing Skee Ball at the arcade down the block instead, or my stick-on tattoo of a skull and crossbones I got for a quarter from a candy dispenser at McDonald's and hid from my mom because, even though it would wash off within a day, I thought she would freak out.

Mollie's been my best friend since we were in the first grade and she was too scared to go into the snake house on a field trip to the zoo. It was the first secret we ever shared. We rode the same bus to school and played together at the neighborhood picnics, but she lived a full block away, which is impossibly far when you're two feet tall. Somehow, that one secret bridged that distance.

I could hear her sniffling behind me as we waited in line, but I was too busy trying to remove a piece of string from the Velcro on my sneaker. By the time I was done, everyone else had already shuffled through the door to the snake house, and it was just me, Mollie, and Carly Morgan's mom left behind. My mom had given me a dollar to spend at the gift shop before I left for school that morning. A dollar couldn't pay for a ream of stickers, much less the stuffed snow leopard I wanted, but it was enough to get an ice cream sandwich from the stand near the giraffes and offer Mollie half as we waited on the bench for our class to come back out.

We sat together on the bus on the way back to school. The next day, she picked me to be her reading partner, and soon, we were sleeping over at each other's houses every Saturday night. It was like that simple piece of string on my shoe had been there for a reason, and now it tied me to her.

I wanted to remind her of that field trip last night. I wanted to say, "Remember the time you were afraid to go into the snake house at the zoo, and I sat with you on a bench eating an ice cream sandwich? Remember how we've been best friends ever since?" But I didn't. Because if one moment could bring us together, maybe another was enough to tear us apart.

We were closer than ever this summer—we hung out at the pool and went to the beach and spent hours walking around the mall just because it was air-conditioned and gave us something to do. But last night, we could have been strangers again, and now it feels like there's this invisible wall between us, and I don't know how it got there or how to tear it down.

Mollie's mom let her invite a bunch of girls from school over for one last sleepover before the end of summer. I grabbed my bag and called out to my parents that I'd see them later and raced through the backyards to Mollie's house like I'd done a thousand times for a thousand sleepovers. But when I got to the door—a door that led to a place that has always felt like home—I didn't recognize it. I froze on her front steps, my bag at my feet, staring at the door knocker with the bronze bird perched above the metal ring, wondering how I'd never noticed it before.

Maybe I had the wrong house. Maybe I was at the wrong door.

Maybe all of this was wrong.

I didn't want to go in. Because if I didn't recognize this door, then maybe I wouldn't recognize anything inside the house, either. This house where I've practically grown up—where I've helped unload the dishwasher and set the table for our families' joint Thanksgiving dinners, where I've played video games with Josh and Justin and sang along with Mr. Engle on his guitar. I know where the garbage bags are kept. I know Mollie's little brother still sleeps with a racecar nightlight even though he's only a year younger than Izzy. I know Mrs. Engle does Tae-Bo in the basement at six thirty every morning because once or twice I've actually joined her.

I know this house like I know my own, the people inside an extended family. All of us—Sam and Josh, me and Mollie, Izzy and Justin… We've grown up in each other's houses, so how could it suddenly feel so foreign, the people inside strangers?

The front door swung open.

"What are you doing?"

Josh. Josh wasn't a stranger. And neither was the golden retriever who slipped past him to lean against my legs, head tilted up and tongue lolling out the side of her mouth, begging to be petted.

Josh glanced at the bag at my feet. "Did you ring the doorbell?"

"No," I said. "I thought about it."

He stared at me, then shook his head—like maybe asking why I'd be ringing the doorbell instead of walking through the front door like I'd done the past ten years was more trouble than it was worth. "They're in the basement," he said. "Dad asked me to get the pizza—you like pineapple, right?"

Maybe it was because it wasn't the same. Maybe it was because it wasn't just me and Mollie playing Barbies in the basement anymore. Instead, it was Mollie and Carly Morgan and Kelly Jacowski and Bethany Willcox listening to music and choreographing dance routines like we were all thirteen again. In a house I'd been going to practically every day since I was six, suddenly I was the one who didn't belong. It was like they had their own language, sharing jokes and stories about what happened last year in Spanish class, and I couldn't say anything because I take French.

I wanted to go home. It sounds so stupid when I write it out like that because here I am, almost sixteen years old, and I was acting like some little kid who just wanted her mom and her dad and her dog. But I did. I wanted to go home.

I went upstairs instead.

Mr. Engle and Josh were watching a baseball game in the living room, and Mrs. Engle was working on a crossword puzzle at the kitchen table. She glanced up and opened her mouth like she wanted to say something, but then only smiled, her eyes filled with a knowing sympathy, and offered me the half-empty bag of potato chips sitting next to her. I scooped up a handful just to show her I was fine, that I didn't feel like talking, and sat beside Josh on the couch, listening to them rant about the game while I fed Ginger crumbs.

At least their dog still felt like home.

I sat there for over an hour. I sat there when Mollie came upstairs, asked me what I was doing, then shrugged when I told her I was watching the game, opened up another bag of chips, and went back down to her friends. I sat there when Mrs. Engle closed her crossword book, dimmed the kitchen light, and went upstairs to bed and when, thirty minutes later, Mr. Engle turned off the TV and followed her. I sat there when Josh turned to me as soon as his dad was out of sight and asked me what was up, and I sat there, not knowing if I could lie to him and tell him everything was fine when it wasn't, so I didn't say anything at all.

I don't remember how it happened. Memory isn't always easy to trust. But somewhere between that silence and Ginger nuzzling my hand with her cold, wet nose, I wanted to cry. Then it wasn't Ginger's nose, but Josh's hand tucked around mine, and I really was crying and curling into a ball and wanting to disappear inside of myself.

I began to say stupid things about how I was so tired, but I knew I wouldn't be able to sleep, and how everything that was so familiar suddenly seemed so foreign, and how Mollie had found new friends and I didn't belong in her life anymore.

And then, just like that, I was asleep. At least, I must have been. Because the next thing I knew, Mr. Engle was coming down the stairs to take Ginger for her morning walk, and there was a blanket draped across my shoulders, and Josh was asleep beside me, our heads resting against the back of the couch and his hand still holding mine.

It was the first time I'd slept through the night in months.

~ *Lia*

Dear Whoever You Are,

I'm back at school for my sophomore year, and it's starting out exactly the same as last year. I don't get it. High school was supposed to feel like a promise—a beautiful, golden promise that everything would change and I would finally be able to grow into myself and show on the outside the person I am on the inside. But all it's been is just another reminder that I'm not that person yet.

I gained ten pounds over the summer. Which isn't a lot, and I'm not even worried about it, except some of Mollie's friends noticed and said something at the sleepover, and suddenly I'm drawn into this world where I think people care too much about what I look like and not enough about the person I actually am. And it makes a difference, you know? It means I'm starting to care too much about what I look like, too.

The thing is—and I guess I can say this to you because I don't even know you—sometimes I can't help but compare myself to the other girls in my class, wondering why I can't be smarter or prettier or funnier like them. And sometimes it makes me want to cry into Bilbo's fur at night because I wonder if it'll always be that way—if I'll always look in the mirror and see my own worst enemy staring back, with my face and my name, following me around like a shadow I can't shake off.

But that's only if I let it, right?

My mom used to say beauty comes from knowing who you are, and all this time I believed her. I don't know. Maybe it was all those years hearing about the human struggle and people rising up in the face of disaster that made me think the other stuff didn't matter in the long run. But then I got to high school, and suddenly it does matter. And now I'm starting to doubt everything, and I don't know what's right anymore.

Right now it feels like the world is just a place where other people get to tell you who you are and what you should be, and basically we're all screwed because we can never be everything everyone wants us to be.

I don't want to change like that. I don't think I should have to. Because I don't think an extra ten pounds is what makes you better or worse as a person. Who cares if I had to go a size up instead of down when I went school shopping with my mom? I don't. So why should they? Why does it matter so much? I mean, why are we even in school and preparing for college so we can get good jobs if everything is based on our appearances, anyway? What does it matter how smart I am or what talents I have—if I had any to begin with—if someone is going to take one look at me and judge me without even speaking to me?

I get first impressions. I get that. But I know these people. I've known them practically my whole life. When I was ten, I was at my dad's clinic when the Jacowski's brought their German Shepherd in after it ran into the back of a pickup truck and knocked itself unconscious. I got some paper and markers from the reception desk and sat in the waiting room with Kelly until her dad came back out and told her the dog would be fine. And I spent the night at Bethany Willcox's house in the third grade after we were paired together for a science project. We made peanut butter cookies from scratch with her mom and little brother and sang along to old Elvis records. And Mollie…

The point is, I know them and they know me. We've all grown up together, so it's not like I'm some kind of surprise to them. It's not like they're meeting me for the first time. So why would they say I "rounded out" over the summer in that tone of voice where you know they're saying something more hateful underneath? What did I ever do to them? Why should whether or not I gained ten pounds over the summer even matter to them when it's no big deal to me?

At least my family is still the same. They've known me my whole life, too, and they don't care what I look like. When I asked them at dinner last night if I looked different to them, Dad shrugged, took another bite of his pork chop, and said, "You look normal to me." Sam snorted, trying to hide a smirk, but Mom's face was full of concern as she asked me why. I slouched further down in my chair, pushing the steamed carrots around the plate with my fork, and told them what Mollie's friends had said at the sleepover. They were quiet for a long moment. When I looked up, Dad was frowning and exchanging glances across the table with my mom.

"The girls in gym class made fun of my braces today," Izzy whispered.

We turned to look at her. Sam cursed under his breath as Mom reached over to stroke her hair, and I promised Izzy she could have any of the clothes that didn't fit me anymore.

Josh and Mollie were already waiting for me in the driveway by the time I put my jacket on to go to school this morning. When I opened the front door, they were watching me, and Mollie's lips were moving, telling him something I couldn't hear.

Josh glanced at me as I tossed my bag in the backseat and slid in next to it. "Did you do something different with your hair?" Our eyes met in the rearview mirror, and I opened my mouth, ready to shout at him or cry or both. "It looks nice," he said.

Then he shifted into reverse and backed out of the driveway. He didn't say another word the whole way to school.

Maybe it doesn't matter to the people who care about you. Maybe all of this—saying it isn't a big deal—is me just trying to convince myself it doesn't matter, either. But it does. Because it hurts.

Maybe I just wish it didn't.

*~ Lia*

**SEPTEMBER 12, 2000**

Dear Whoever You Are,

Here's a question for you: how do you know you're good at something unless the world tells you? When people say you're "talented," what does it mean aside from the fact that their opinion is shaping what you like and who you are, based solely on how good you are at it?

"What brings this up?" my doctor asked this afternoon.

"My English teacher wants me to join the literary arts journal at school."

"What's that, a club?"

I shrugged. "Yeah, kind of."

"And you like English and writing, right? No problems there?"

He meant no failed tests like last year, even though last year I was having all those problems sleeping and it was making my head feel funny—like everything I knew was just out of reach, my fingertips skimming the answers but never able to grasp them.

"I like Mrs. Giudieri," I answered.

There's something about English with Mrs. Giudieri that's different from my other classes. It's not the fact that she's so passionate about everything because my math teacher is the same way about numbers, and we like listening to him talk because it makes us feel like we can figure out forever if we just solve for infinity. And it's not because of what we're reading, because I love *The Lottery* and hate *The Tell-Tale Heart*, but it's something more. It's like I'm always on the verge of naming something unnamable, and every day I walk into that class, I can't help but wonder if that's the day I'll figure out what it is.

We're writing our own short stories this week. I used to write poetry on the backs of wallpaper samples when I was little—small, stupid rhymes my mom still keeps in an old copy paper box with the rest of my school stuff— but I've never written anything like this before. You know, really creating something. I like the idea that everything I put on the page comes from me, from my imagination, and it doesn't even matter whether or not I get a good grade because someone else will be reading it. For that one moment, they'll be picturing what I pictured and feeling what I felt. It's sort of intoxicating, the way you can fill up a page with images and thoughts like that. If I believed in magic, I'd think writing was a spell.

That sounds stupid, though.

Doesn't it?

"Not stupid." My doctor smiled. "It's nice that you feel that way about something. Too many people go their entire lives not feeling that way about anything."

"What about you?" I asked. "Do you feel that way about anything?"

He shifted in his chair, the leather squeaking against the brush of fabric from his clothes. "I probably did, once."

"So, what changed?"

"I guess I did." He paused. "It's easy to lose the magic as you get older. You stop seeing things for what they are and start seeing them for what you want them to be."

"And that's bad?"

"Well," he shrugged, "it's dangerous." He cleared his throat and glanced down at the notepad in his lap. It was blank, except for a couple of swirls I saw him doodling earlier. I was beginning to think he used it as a safety blanket—just something to have nearby, something to do while we talked. "How did it make you feel when Mrs. Guery—"

"Giudieri," I corrected him.

"Right. How did it make you feel when she asked you to join?"

Proud. It made me feel proud. When she pulled me aside before the bell rang and asked me to be a part of the editorial staff, it was more like a request than a suggestion, and I carried that with me all the way home.

You don't get a lot of chances to feel proud in high school. Okay, yes, you feel happy when you ace the test you studied really hard for, but I think that's more like relief. I'm talking about the kind of proud that shows you and the world who you are, like last week when Mr. Humphrey dropped his books in the hallway and his papers scattered all over the tile floor. Because he's kinda eccentric, everyone else just laughed and walked past him, but Mollie and I stopped to help him gather everything up.

Or the time I yelled at a bunch of seniors to quit being assholes to Mimi Liang. I had the locker across from her last year. She was crouched down, getting books out of the bottom shelf, when three seniors walked past and pulled the strap of her backpack. No one else was around to see her fall, sprawled on her back in the hallway—it was just them and me and Mimi—but they laughed and slapped each other's hands and kept walking, and out of nowhere, I yelled at them to knock it off.

I may have said something else.

The thing is, I didn't even realize the words were coming out of my mouth. But they did. They must have. Because the seniors stopped and looked back at me, and I thought they were going to say something, but they didn't.

Mimi didn't thank me or smile at me. She just gathered her books and walked away. It's not like I wanted her to—I mean, I didn't even know what I was doing when I did it—but I remember that day because it made me feel good to stand up for something, and I had this fleeting thought about how that was the kind of person I wanted to be.

That's the kind of proud I'm talking about. The kind that helps you figure out what kind of person you are or, better yet, who you want to be. But does the world get a say in that, too? I know who I'm not, does that count? I know I'll never get a trophy for scoring a goal because I'm less than average when it comes to sports, and while I can hold my own with Sammy at the dinner table, I'll never get a ribbon for winning a debate because the thought of talking in front of a crowd makes my mouth go dry.

So what's left for someone like me?

Isabella's the artist in the family. Two years ago, my parents gave her a professional art kit for Christmas with watercolors and oil pastels and a sketchbook, and she's pretty brilliant at it. And Sam takes after my dad when it comes to sports—he was in Little League when he was younger, went to states with the swim team when he was a junior, and was on the soccer team with Josh when they won the regional championship his senior year. They don't have to think about whether or not they're good at anything—they just know they are, and they become who they are because of it: the artist and the athlete.

And me. Just Lia. I'm just a girl who likes to look at paintings but can never figure out how they transferred the picture in their head to a canvas on a wall. Just someone who likes the idea of team spirit but would rather spend her time on the bench than on a field.

So when Mrs. Giudieri said she thought I was talented when it came to writing, I felt proud, like this could be my thing. Because I love to write, but I never thought about whether or not I was actually any good at it. Writing was just another way to figure out what I was thinking or feeling or whatever—I never thought anyone would actually want to read those stories outside of getting a grade.

Like you and these letters. Who knows if you're even reading them. But if you are because you want to… Maybe that says something.

I'm not an artist or an athlete because I can't paint or throw a ball for crap. And maybe I'm not even a writer just because I like to write and one person says I'm actually okay at it. But maybe that one person's opinion makes it worth exploring, when you might have otherwise given up.

I said yes. I'm officially on staff for *Typescript* and have my first meeting Monday after school.

"And how do you feel about being on staff?" he asked, but I had a feeling he already knew.

"I'm nervous," I answered. "I'm excited."

And I think Mrs. Giudieri may have just changed my life.

~ *Lia*

**SEPTEMBER 28, 2000**

Dear Whoever You Are,

Hearing your parents fight is the worst feeling in the world. They can yell at you all they want because you're pretty much immune to it by this point, but when that's directed at each other, it's all you can do to keep breathing. You're not supposed to be eavesdropping in the first place, so you can't do anything except sit in the doorway of your bedroom and listen to their angry voices filter up the stairs.

That's where we are tonight, as I'm writing you this letter—we're sitting on the carpet in the doorways of our rooms. I'm leaning against the doorframe, and Izzy's doodling on her cast with a collection of colored Sharpies, and Sam's hanging his head so it looks like he's sleeping, but every once in a while, when Mom or Dad raise their voice, he'll shake his head and exhale loudly through his nose.

We can't hear everything, but we catch stray phrases like "so much debt" and "partner at the clinic" and "Izzy's hospital bill"—just enough to conclude that my sister fracturing her wrist on the playground this afternoon is probably what led to this argument, but it's not what's keeping them there.

I'm watching Izzy draw hibiscus and water lilies and rose bushes on her cast, blending them together so they look like some kind of ethereal floral landscape, and I'm awed at how she can transform something so broken into a work of art. Next to her, Sam stretches out his legs and leans his head against the wall. He won't look me in the eye, so I can't tell what he's thinking. I wish I could tell what he's thinking.

Then again, maybe I already know. Maybe that's how it is with brothers and sisters. You don't have to say anything when your mom calls with instructions to find something for dinner because they'll be at the hospital a little while longer. You just order a pizza with your sister's favorite toppings and chip in your own money without a second thought. And when you're trying to rest or do your homework or watch TV in your room, and you hear your parents' raised voices travel up the stairs, you open your bedroom door—and they open theirs—and you look at each other and sit down in the doorway...

And there you are. You don't have to say anything in that moment because there's nothing to say. All you need to know is they're sitting on the floor with you, and that's enough.

My mom's crying. We all freeze. Isabella's pen is pressed against her cast, the ink expanding, ruining the canvas she's created. Sam and I glance at each other, and I ask him what they're saying, but he just leans further out his door towards the stairs. Izzy scoots closer to me and whispers that she heard Mom and Dad talking in the hospital—that Mom was passed over as department chair, and now she's wondering if she should leave teaching altogether.

I have to ask her three times if she's sure she heard them correctly, and when I start to ask again, she stomps back to her room and slams the door. Downstairs, I can hear my dad's voice, low and comforting, and I imagine he has his arms around my mom, stroking her hair like I saw him do at Grandpa Lawson's funeral. It's the only other time I've seen my mom cry.

I take it back, what I said before. Hearing my mom cry is the worst feeling in the world. I expected it when my grandpa died because he was her father, but she's crying now because she didn't get a job she wanted or because Izzy broke her arm or because they're having financial trouble or any number of things—or maybe all of these things—and it makes me realize how little I actually know her, to never expect her to cry like that.

Sam stands, and I watch him rest his hand on the banister. I think he's going to say something, or maybe go downstairs and hug my mom the way I want to, but he turns around and walks back to his room. A second later, I see the familiar flicker of light from the TV beneath his closed door.

Now I'm just sitting here, alone in the hallway, writing it all down on a piece of notebook paper. I think about how

I've shared more with you than I ever have with my mom, and I'm the one who wants to cry.

Because I don't know who's more of a stranger now: you—

or her.

~ *Lia*

OCTOBER 16, 2000

Dear Whoever You Are,

It's hot for the middle of October. Last year, it snowed on Halloween, but now, everyone's outside in short sleeves, and some girls even came to school wearing their flip-flops like it's still summer. Everyone is clinging to the warm air because they know what's coming—a winter that starts off beautiful and magical but that quickly grows dark and cold in a way that makes you want to stay inside and hibernate until April.

No one is hibernating now. Bilbo's lying on his side in a patch of sunshine by the open front door. Every once in a while, when a lone jogger or a trio of mothers pushing baby strollers pass by the house, he'll sit up and sniff at the air and follow them with his eyes, but he doesn't bark anymore. He's getting too old for that now. Instead, he watches them through the screen door, and I wonder what he's thinking. I wonder if he really longs to get up and howl like he used to—a sound that's more whine than warning.

Maybe he imagines himself chasing them down for a belly rub, remembering how strangers used to fawn over him when he was a puppy. Sometimes, I'll see his paws twitching in his sleep, and it makes me think he's running in his dreams. I wonder if he misses it—if he misses running—and the thought makes me so sad because he's such a good boy that I always stop whatever I'm doing and scratch the scruff on his backside until he's fully on his back, panting and smiling and happy to be right where he is again.

Sam and Josh are shooting hoops outside. I can hear their voices and the occasional thud of the ball against the backboard from my place at the kitchen counter, where I'm supposed to be doing my math homework, but I'm writing you this letter instead. I'll have to ask my doctor if he thinks this is some kind of act of rebellion—writing letters that will be tucked away in a plastic lunchbox and buried beneath a pile of dirt with the hopes that it will be found by some stranger far off into the future instead of doing what I'm supposed to be doing. It's just—this feels more important right now. And I probably can't ever explain it to him or my parents or my teachers in a way that makes sense to them—"Sorry, Mr. Moore. I didn't do my homework because I was too busy writing about how much I love my dog and wondering about the state of the world in a hundred years."

Because that would go over super well.

But it is. It's important. I don't know why, but it feels like I have this connection to something bigger than myself, and these letters—writing to you—is my way of figuring out what that is.

My world doesn't make sense. And I don't know if it's because that's just how the world is or if it ever ends up making sense at all, but I want it to. I desperately want to understand it, and these letters at least give me a glimpse of *something*.

At least that's something.

Sam and Josh just came inside. Their cheeks are flushed, and sweat is dripping from their hair. They grab two Gatorades from the fridge and gulp them down in half a second, then toss the empty bottles in the sink. I caught Josh glancing at my books as he walked past me, but I'm keeping my head down because he's only wearing a pair of mesh shorts, and I'm pretty sure my face is just as red as theirs.

Sorry. I probably shouldn't have written that. It's just that I'm here, furiously scribbling in my notebook, because they're still in the kitchen, rooting through the pantry and talking about their old soccer team and the way things were when Sam was in high school. And I'm trying not to listen in, but they're *right there,* and I can't help but hear what they're saying. I just want to yell at them to go back outside or put on a shirt—or don't put on a shirt, whatever—and, God, I'm becoming like those girls Mollie hangs out with, aren't I? What is wrong with me? This is *Josh.* We've eaten Thanksgiving dinner together since I was twelve, been assigned to the same bus stop since elementary school, and played together at the neighborhood picnic since we were all in diapers. I've known him since before Mollie and I were even best friends.

And now I want to look at him, but I'm too embarrassed to look at him.

I'm pathetic.

I keep willing them to leave, but they're ripping open the wrappers of an entire package of string cheese and talking about how Sam wants to transfer from the community college to a state school next year, and I have to force myself not to look up, even though I want to. Sam never wants to talk about school when Mom and Dad ask him, and I don't know why he's talking about it now, right in front of me, but it makes me feel special, like he trusts me, like maybe he thinks of me as more than his kid sister.

"You gonna try for a scholarship?" I hear Sam ask.

"I dunno. I think I'm done with soccer after this year."

My head jerks up at Josh's answer, and the words fly out of my mouth before I can stop them. "But you love soccer!"

They both turn to me, like they're surprised to see me, like they've forgotten I'm even there. Something about that hurts, but I don't say anything. I just go back to writing this stupid letter. Josh is quiet now, staring at the empty food wrappers in his hand.

"C'mon," Sam says, and I watch them go outside, Bilbo slipping out the door with them.

I can't help but think I've said something wrong. I can't help but wish I could take it all back.

~ *Lia*

## OCTOBER 24, 2000

Dear Whoever You Are,

The trees looked like skeletons in the dark. A few brown leaves still clung to their bare branches, but even more were scooped into piles along the curb where they'd already begun to decay. A few of our neighbors had their Halloween decorations up—carved pumpkins waiting on front stoops and cloth ghosts hanging from lampposts. One yard was scattered with fake gravestones, and I couldn't escape the shiver that ran up my arms when I saw their silhouettes, even though I knew they were nothing more than recycled wood.

Beside me, Josh glanced my way but didn't say anything, and I rolled my eyes and called out to Izzy not to get too far ahead of us. I didn't really care—we'd walked down this street a thousand times before—but I didn't like how quiet he was being, and I had to break the silence somehow.

Izzy and I went over to the Engles' after dinner tonight—Justin had a new video game he wanted to show her, and Mollie and I had to finish some homework for school. We're not in any of the same classes this year, but we have the same chemistry teacher who likes to talk like we have any idea what we're doing. We don't. Even Colby Donahue, who's practically a genius, seems just as clueless as the rest of us.

We spent an hour flipping through our notes and books at the kitchen table, trying to make sense of what we were supposed to be learning, before her mom stepped in and helped us piece it all together. When we were finished, I yelled down the basement steps for Izzy and shoved my books in my backpack. Josh must have heard me because he came downstairs, grabbed his jacket off the hook in the entryway, and offered to walk us home. I told him he didn't have to—we could cut through the backyards like we always did—but he said it was dark outside and he didn't mind.

I stared at him, then exchanged glances with Mollie, who raised her eyebrows and said she'd see me tomorrow before taking her books upstairs. When I turned to Mrs. Engle, she shook her head and hid a smile behind her hand; Mr. Engle changed the channel on the TV.

"What's wrong with you?" I asked Josh. Because not once in the years our families have been friends has he ever offered to take us home.

He sighed loudly and held the front door open. "Just shut up and go before I change my mind."

It was the last thing we said to each other the whole way down the street. We hadn't said much since the sleepover. We hadn't said much since that day in my kitchen. And now, here we were again, walking home in silence like this was some chore he was forced to do, only nobody asked him to do it.

I kept trying to think of things to say to him, but he wouldn't even look at me, and the weirder he was being, the angrier I was getting. I wanted to tell him to stop acting like he was some stranger, and what was going on with him, anyway, and why did he have to walk us home today of all days?

That's when he stopped. Just stopped walking. I didn't even notice until I was already a few steps ahead of him, and Izzy doubled-back to ask what was wrong. I glanced at the street around us—at the houses with the fall wreaths on their doors and mums in baskets on the porch steps—and it all seemed so unfamiliar. For a split-second, I felt lost—like I didn't recognize the street without him beside me. But then I turned around, and he was there, standing underneath one of the streetlamps near the Jacobey's front yard, the light stretching across the pavement in a sort of semi-circle that reached the tips of my sneakers.

Something struck me about that. I can't remember what, but I didn't want to be outside that circle of light without him. So I stepped closer, tugging the sleeve of Izzy's jacket to bring her along with me.

He shifted his weight and crossed his arms but didn't say a word. I started to tell him, fine, we could walk the rest of the way without him, but he started talking about the Fourth of July and how I had practically disappeared once the fireworks began. It caught me so off-guard, I could only blink and stare at him and wonder why on Earth he was bringing this up now, standing on the edge of a darkened street in the middle of October.

"Why?" he kept asking.

Why what? Why was I afraid? Why did I hide out in Mollie's room instead of staying outside with everyone else? Why did I have 911 on speed dial and a fire extinguisher beside the front door? Hell if I knew. Do you ever really know why you're afraid? I just was.

I told him this. I told him that I didn't know, but he kept insisting that I did. Izzy was as quiet as I've ever seen her, her head turning back and forth between us like she wasn't sure when this started or where it would end. I thought about how we might be upsetting her, so I yelled at him—something like "who cares" or "does it even matter?"—until hot tears began to sting my eyes. But if he saw me cry, it would only make it worse, so I turned and stomped away instead.

He caught up to me quickly. He reached for my arm and asked me to slow down a minute in a voice that wasn't angry, but soft—like a plea—and unlike anything I'd ever heard from him before. I was so surprised that I did stop, which made him pause, and I thought, *here we go again*. But he ducked his head and reached into his back pocket, pulling out a lighter and a couple of sparklers while Izzy squealed in excitement, and I just stared at him, confused.

"They've been your favorite since the third grade," he said. "I know you never got the chance this year."

It's funny how out of everything we yelled to each other tonight, that's what I remember most. Not his offer to walk us home, not shouting beneath the lamplight, not even how he asked me to wait when I began to walk away. It was how he knew the sparklers were my favorite and the way his eyes seemed to plead as much as his words, even though he wouldn't look at me for long.

He handed one to Izzy, who giggled and skipped down the street, the sparks trailing behind her like a tiny meteor shower. I couldn't keep the smile from spreading across my lips, even though I wanted to be angry with him for being so weird about everything in the first place.

Josh and I traced words and spun patterns and wrote our secrets in fading script on the air until the last spark hissed and sputtered and burned out, and we were left alone, grinning stupidly at each other in the dark.

"Happy birthday, Lia," he said.

Then he shrugged, like pilfering sparklers from the

Fourth of July stash in his garage was no big deal, picked my backpack off the ground, and walked me the rest of the way home.

~ *Lia*

**NOVEMBER 7, 2000**

Dear Whoever You Are,

He smelled faintly of cigarette smoke. It hid behind the vanilla air freshener and lingered with the burning leaves that pushed through the open window from a farm a half mile away. It trailed after him as he walked past me to his desk, and I imagined I actually saw it, clinging to the collar of his dress shirt, settling to the couch cushions, and staining his books so that one day, far from now, someone walking through a secondhand bookshop would pause and skim the pages, wondering at the man who let his words become so tainted.

"You smoke?" I asked.

He raised his eyebrows, then glanced away sheepishly, slid open his top desk drawer, and pulled out a tin of breath mints. "Force of habit from the army."

He popped one in his mouth, then offered them to me. I leaned over and took one, some part of me wondering if I was sharing his vice, another part painfully aware of how he looked to me now—more real than he ever did before.

"You were a soldier?" I don't know why that surprised me. He didn't look like a soldier, with his shaggy blond hair and five o'clock shadow. But maybe that's what soldiers left behind when the war was over. "When?"

"I was young," he said. "Too young."

"Did you—Were you…" I didn't know how to ask him about it, didn't know if I had a right to any part of his life, even though he was ordered to scrutinize every piece of mine.

He nodded but wouldn't look me in the eye. "The war that was." His voice was filled with something rancid and raw, like a memory choking its way out. "The war that never should have been."

I followed his gaze to the window, my eyes settling on the dark blue ashtray that rested on the ledge. I imagined him standing there, watching the sun begin to dip behind the horizon while the tractor from the neighboring farm rumbled over the terrain towards the barn, kicking up dust from the empty field behind it. The cigarette would burn between his fingers until he remembered it was there, then he'd take one long drag, drop it in the ashtray, and walk away from what he wanted to forget.

I looked away.

"My mom talks about it like that, too," I said quietly.

We didn't speak for the rest of the hour.

*~ Lia*

Dear Whoever You Are,

I never noticed the carpet in his office before. I feel like I should have. Because if I could notice everything else the minute I stepped through the doorway that first day last fall—a pile of fiction books stacked so high in a corner by his desk they were beginning to lean, the tangle of electrical cords attached to a power strip by the couch, the empty box of tissues that has been sitting on his desk all year—then maybe I should have noticed the carpet. It's the same kind of industrial carpet they have in the library at school—the kind that's coarse and thin and one step up from walking on tile. The kind that's meant to quiet, not comfort.

The words hung suspended between us, his last question floating around in my head, trying to find some escape or refuge—whichever came first. I kept my head down, my gaze fixed on a small patch of carpet by the desk leg. For a second, I thought I was seeing things, and I squinted and shifted in the chair so I could lean forward and study the colored threads that wove their way through a field of gray. I wished I was wrong—wished for once something could be exactly what it appeared to be—but there they were, flecks of blue and white and red creating a haphazard pattern, a cloud of color whirling at my feet like a warning that you never know when the storm might strike.

"Amelia?"

I don't want to talk about it. I don't want to talk about it. It happened so long ago—it's been a full year already, so why did we have to talk about it? Not now, not when I'm not ready, when I don't want to...

"Are you still having trouble sleeping?"

My heartbeat quieted and I breathed out, grateful for the change in his voice, now gentle and patient. It was a lead-in question—I knew all about those. I wasn't answering the one he wanted me to—the one that led us there—so he was trying again, his words more calculated, more tactful. We were back to being two people having a simple conversation, navigating our way around the months of small talk and details that would eventually bring us full circle.

"Yes," I said. "No. Sometimes."

I glanced down at my hand, at the silver mood ring Mollie and I had picked up at the boardwalk this past summer, on that wish-filled day where I thought I belonged to forever. It was just a small, cheap mold of metal and stone, but I liked that the blue seemed to match both sky and ocean, and I had this fleeting thought that maybe I could capture the timelessness I felt on the beach—even if only a glimpse of it—in a twelve-dollar ring. Now, the stone had clouded over into a muddy orange, and I twisted it around on my finger and enclosed it in my palm.

"What about the night you fell asleep on the couch?" he asked.

"A fluke, I guess."

I didn't want it to be. I wanted that night to mean something. I still think about it all the time, replaying the moment in my head like a broken record. I can still see the sunlight struggling through the curtains as the night morphed into morning, the sleeping clinging to the last, fading memories of their dreams. I can still hear Ginger's nails dancing on the kitchen linoleum, waiting for Mr. Engle to slip on her leash and open the door. I still feel Josh right there, right next to me, his chest rising and falling in rhythm, his hand heavy around mine.

The more I can remember, the closer I think I can hold onto the memory of that moment before I slipped my hand away from his and snuck back down to the basement. Each night, I fall asleep imagining unspoken secrets written on the air with stolen sparklers. Every morning, I wonder if dreams are enough.

They never are. Because I always wake up—always.

"It's not that I'm not getting any sleep," I explained. "It's just that I never feel like I'm getting enough."

"It makes it difficult to concentrate." It wasn't a question, but I nodded anyway. "It's why you failed your history test—"

That damn history test.

"—and your math test—"

And my math test.

"—and your biology quiz?"

Yep, that one, too.

"What happened that night?" he asked.

That night. That night…

I don't want to tell you. I don't want to write those words here. I don't want to put this letter in my time capsule because what if you read it? What will you think of me? Everything that came before will be erased, and it will be just this—this picture of me you keep in your mind, and I'm so much more than just one night…

That one bad night.

I'd snuggled beneath my covers like usual, the sheets folded into my fist and tucked beneath my chin in the same way I've been falling asleep all my life. The room was dark, except for the blue lights of the stereo on my dresser, and the half-moon peeked through the window and cast a trail of shadows across the carpet. Bilbo was stretched across the foot of my bed, and I scooted over to make more room for him. He heaved a sigh and tucked himself into the backs of my legs, and soon, I was listening to his heavy breathing that would usually send me to sleep like a lullaby.

Except that night, I was wide awake.

I stared at the digital clock on my nightstand, counting the seconds until the numbers changed again and again. Time kept ticking by, passing from minute to minute until the TV in my parents' room clicked off, and Sam came and went to the bathroom down the hall, and the house settled into silence once more. I'd tried reading one more chapter of *The Bell Jar* for school, tried watching one more re-run of *I Love Lucy*, tried flipping through the pages of my biology book for one more review of my notes before my quiz, but it was like my eyes didn't want to close.

I rolled onto my back and stared at the ceiling, tracing the sticker constellations that would fade in the daylight, and willed myself not to look at the clock. But it was all I could do. All I wanted was four hours of sleep, three hours of sleep, one more hour of sleep before my alarm went off, but it was like the harder I tried, the more my mind kept racing with all these thoughts and dates and algebra equations that probably weren't even real equations but a mismatch of numbers and letters my mind made up.

I was so tired. I was so tired, and I just wanted to close my eyes and sink into my dreams and make the world go away like everyone else who was wrapped up in their beds. But the silence was so loud, taunting me that I was still awake, and the darkness just made it worse.

I thought about counting sheep, but that was stupid, and going downstairs to drink warm milk and honey, but that sounded gross, and burning the lavender candle my mom got from Aunt Kathy and Uncle Jim for her birthday years ago, but what would that do, really? I thought about grabbing a bottle of vodka or gin from the liquor cabinet in the living room, but I've only ever had wine at Christmas and a Zima at New Year's, and I didn't like the way those made me feel, anyway.

I thought about the leftover pain medication from when I had my tonsils out the winter before last—thought about the way my mom had tucked one of Grandma Lenelli's afghans around me on the couch after I arrived home from the hospital. The medicine had knocked me out, and when I woke up, I forgot for a minute that my throat even hurt in the first place.

I just wanted to sleep—the kind of sleep where you wake up so refreshed you forget you were even asleep at all. The memory of the last time I'd slept like that was so strong, it was enough to get me out of bed and root through the medicine basket underneath the bathroom sink. I'd barely used any of the prescription, and the pills piled into my hand and spread across my palm.

I was so tired.

I was so tired.

You have to understand, I was so tired.

And I was desperate. And I was lonely. And I didn't want to be all three of those things at once, especially not at four in the morning.

I couldn't remember if I should take one or two, and what difference would it make if I took three or four? Five or six and I'd fall asleep and not wake up until I was ready and able to function in the world again like a normal human being. Maybe that's what I needed—just a few more than two...

"What are you doing?"

I hadn't seen Izzy there, standing in the doorway, and when I spun around, the medicine spilled from my hand and scattered across the floor, into the grooves in the tile and beside the toilet and under the sink. I started to cry and scream at her, and I fell to my knees, desperate to pick up every last tablet, counting them like I'd counted the seconds on the clock because if I missed just one, I thought I'd never get to sleep again.

"What happened next, Lia?" My doctor leaned forward, his voice still gentle, still patient.

I twisted the ring around and around on my finger. I didn't want to look at it, didn't want to see whatever it had to tell me, so I stared at the patch of carpet below my sneakers, at the storm that kept brewing in those colored strands.

"Sam woke up," I said. "He must have heard me yelling because he stumbled out of his room, half asleep and cursing..."

Until he took one look at me on my knees on the bathroom floor and ordered Izzy to get my mom and dad.

"How many did you take?" He crouched in front of me, his hands gripping my shoulders and shaking me with force. I could only stare at him, my voice raw from screaming, my eyes bloodshot from crying. "How many did you take, Lia?" Sam had shouted at me.

"How many did you take, Lia?" My doctor asked me.

All of them.

~ *Lia*

PART TWO

DECEMBER 5, 2000

Dear Whoever You Are,

There's a part of me that wishes I never told you. Then maybe you wouldn't think what my parents and doctors thought—even though I was telling them the truth—and you wouldn't have to wish you'd never dug up this time capsule and started reading these letters. Because I bet that's what you're thinking right now...

It's what I'm thinking right now.

I was in the hospital for two days after that, hooked up to an IV that dripped saline into my veins while nurses patted my arm and checked my blood pressure and doctors frowned and flipped through my chart and asked me the same question a thousand different ways.

"Why do you do that?" I asked my doctor. I was sitting on the paisley couch now, leaning against the armrest. He'd pulled his leather chair around the side of the desk so it no longer served as a boundary between us, like my finally telling him what happened had helped us cross this bridge where we were no longer strangers, and definitely not friends, but somewhere in between.

He froze and looked up from the notepad where he was doodling misshapen circles and slanted stars. "Do what?" The words were drawn out, like he was testing them.

"Ask the same question a million different ways." I shifted on the couch, tucking my leg beneath me. "I remember the doctors kept asking the same question over and over like I was supposed to have a different answer. You do that, too."

He tilted his head. "Do I?"

"Sometimes."

He chuckled and rubbed his jawline. "I think it's all about communication," he said finally. "Words are left to interpretation—if there are a thousand ways to ask a question, there are a thousand ways to respond. Sometimes people divulge only small fragments of themselves at a time. It's up to us to piece the story together—kinda like a puzzle."

"You think I'm a puzzle?"

I didn't like that. It didn't seem right. I didn't want to be a piece of something, I wanted to be whole, on my own. And if someone wanted to get to know me, then I wanted them to get to know the complete me.

Even if I don't entirely know who that is yet.

He opened his mouth like he wanted to say something else, then shut it again and glanced down at the notepad, the tip of the pen resting against the paper but not creating anything. "What happened next, Lia?"

No one seemed to know what to do with me. That's what happened next. I wasn't acting out or transforming into some alternate version of myself. I wasn't trying to escape from whatever problems they thought I had, and I definitely wasn't trying to hurt myself. When they finally realized that—when my parents saw I was still Amelia and there might actually be something wrong with me—I think they were relieved.

The doctors ordered a bunch of bloodwork and relented to a mild sedative that helped me sleep through the night. When I woke up the next morning to a warm breakfast tray beside me and my mom flipping through a magazine in a nearby chair, I felt normal and human and not like this zombie that had been walking through the world half-awake. The tests came back clear, so they sent me home with a bottle of melatonin that has only somewhat helped since, a pamphlet on stress management I promptly shoved in the back of a notebook and forgot about, and a referral to a psychologist.

"That's you," I said to my doctor. He didn't return my smile.

Except for a few questions, my friends acted normal when I went back to school. Josh kept passing by my locker between classes, even though he didn't say much, and Mollie and Bethany helped me catch up on everything I'd missed. But there was a confusion that lingered beneath their smiles—like this one incident had defined me and they didn't know what to think of me anymore. I couldn't blame them, but that doesn't mean it didn't hurt, and I'm still not sure if everything's the same.

"It wasn't just one incident, though, was it?"

I stared at him, glanced at the folder on his desk that was becoming thick with written summaries of our sessions. A full year of coming here, to this office. A full year of conversations and telling him how I hadn't been sleeping—all of it leading to last week when I finally described the night the world wouldn't turn off.

"It's not just the sleep anymore," he said. "That was last year, this is today. What happened today?"

I sank back against the cushions. If I was a puzzle, then all the pieces he had helped me figure out about myself—all those pieces we had spent the past year putting into place— were shattered once more, scattered across the landscape of my life.

"What happened in school today," he tried again.

Today I ran away.

~ *Lia*

## DECEMBER 6, 2000

Dear Whoever You Are,

I can't help but wonder how much of our evolution is based on survival of the fittest and how much is based on pure dumb luck. Because if survival is based on basic human physiology and our fight or flight reflex like everyone claims it is, then I was doing exactly what our ancestors have done for millions and millions of years when I ran out of English class yesterday.

Just trying to save my own life.

Except when you're sixteen, that looks an awful lot like skipping school, which means detention and a trip to the principal's office, where she tried to figure out why such a good student would run out of class like that.

Good question. I wish I knew.

It came out of nowhere, the heaviness in my chest grow-ing deeper as the second-hand ticked by on the clock on the wall. One minute, I was listening to Mrs. Giudieri talk about James Joyce; the next, her words were becoming so distant and jumbled, I could have been underwater, and for a second, I thought I really might be drowning. I stared at the open book on my desk, trying to distract myself with someone else's story, but the line repeated itself, like it was hyper-imposed on my brain:

*"He lived at a little distance from his body."*

I didn't understand what I was reading. I understood it too well.

*"He lived at a little distance from his body."*

The words blended and blurred together, and no matter how I tried to pick them apart and focus on each one at a time, they merged into groups of letters that lost all sense. My heart began to beat faster as I fought for meaning, and I inhaled sharply, but the deeper the breath I took, the less air there seemed to be in the world, and suddenly it felt like there wasn't enough air for everyone. My heart raced against the seconds on the clock as my palms grew cold and clammy, my mind screaming the only word I knew: "Run!"

*Run.*

So I did.

I ran.

I nearly tipped over my desk as I bolted out of my seat and raced through the halls and threw open the front doors. I would have run all the way home, but my heart was already threatening to beat outside my chest, and my lungs burned as they fought for air, and I started to cry—full-out bawling right next to Benji Harris' Honda Accord. I crouched down and leaned against the back tire, gulping in mouthfuls of cold air, only to end up releasing a series of sobs instead.

The bell rang twice while I was out there—a warning that class was over and I was monumentally screwed. I imagined my notebook, still on the floor, the pages creased from the fall. My pen had probably rolled away, lost forever in some forgotten corner of the room.

I didn't want to walk back into that school. I just wanted to pretend my life was all just a bad dream because that's how it felt right then—like I was walking through a dream, and I didn't know whether it or I was real. I was numb— every last bit of everything inside of me had been wrung out like a sponge, and I had nothing left.

*"He lived at a little distance from his body."*

The secretary called me into the office as soon as I walked through the doors, telling me my dad was already on his way in that disapproving tone of voice that let me know I was in serious trouble. She didn't have to say anything else. I could tell by her frown she thought I was just another delinquent. To her, I was probably some overdramatic kid who was too caught up in her own self to care about obeying the rules. Maybe I ran out of school because I didn't want to take a test or I broke up with my boyfriend. Maybe I ran out just for kicks or because I was rebelling.

Never mind the fear that threatened to choke me. Never mind that the only thing my mind could focus on was one word, over and over and over again. Never mind that the room felt too small, and I was too close to suffocating, and no one could ever reach me from the depths where I was drowning. Never mind that none of those things made any sense even to me, but in that moment, if I didn't leave that room—that building—and get outside, I wouldn't survive.

Never mind any of that. She was right. I did it just because. Because I *wanted* to feel humiliated and called into the principal's office and have my dad leave work and come down to the school all worried like that. And, yes. I want to go see that guidance counselor who doesn't know me, but he thinks he knows me because, apparently, we're all the same. And if one sixteen year old cuts class because she wants to smoke a joint behind the dumpsters, then that must be what I was trying to do, too.

I need you to know what really happened. I need you to know I wasn't trying to sneak out so I could smoke up. I was just trying to save my own life.

One breath at a time.

~ *Lia*

**JANUARY 2, 2001**

Dear Whoever You Are,

I was looking north. Past the white-washed walls and navy-striped curtains of his office, past the windows whose glass panes would be cold to the touch, past the parking lot where minivans sat next to Mustangs, their heaters running at full blast, and past farmland that dipped into the valley before rising again like it was trying to race the sunset. North on the highway, north past the high school, north through the winding streets of my neighborhood where, in my backyard, buried two feet beneath the soil, lay everything I've ever wanted to say.

I was looking north because I didn't want to look at him.

"Do you think it was a panic attack?" I asked my doctor, threading my fingers through the fringe on one of the throw pillows on the couch.

It's what Dr. Denlinger had called it at my latest visit. He'd frowned when he saw me back in his office, asked me if I was still seeing my psychologist, then, after checking my heart and eyes and ears and everything else that didn't have anything to do with anything, he scribbled down the name of some anxiety medication, ripped the sheet from the prescription pad, and handed it to me.

"I mean, it could have been a panic attack, right?"

My doctor had the notepad and pen in his lap, sketching swirls and squares in the upper-left corner of the page, and I reached into my backpack and pulled out a notebook and pen and started doing the same. He paused and watched me, a half-smile turning up the corners of his mouth. Then he stood, pulled out a pack of colored pencils from his desk drawer, and tossed them onto the empty couch cushion beside me.

"It's good for the mind—doodling," he said. "There was a study a few years back that showed it improves brain function and helps retain memories."

"Is that why you draw while we talk? To retain other people's memories?"

He froze and looked up, tilting his head like he was seeing something for the first time. Not me—he wasn't seeing me for the first time, but something about me. It was like he was straddling the past and the present, and I was the one keeping him there in that room. One blink, and he would become someone else, someone I never knew, someone long ago.

"Sometimes it's easier to listen to other people's stories than to remember your own," he said quietly. He cleared his throat and brushed the tip of the pen against the page again. "Yes, to answer your question. I think it was a panic attack."

I opened the pack of colored pencils and tilted the box so they slid out of the packaging. The tips were filed down from use, and they were grouped by color like his books. I wondered if he always put them back in that order.

I'm not an artist like Izzy. I don't know anything about colors or drawing—my daisies always droop like they're wilting, the hearts nothing more than disjointed half circles that could never beat a pulse. But he was right. There was something comforting about the movement of the pencil and the way the color shaded the empty space between the lines, and I wondered if this was how it felt for Izzy when she painted—to create something that was hers and hers alone, no matter what it looked like in the end.

"I felt like I couldn't breathe," I admitted, keeping my head down and my eyes on the paper in my lap. "I didn't think I would ever be able to breathe again unless I was home safe with my parents and Sam and Izzy and Bilbo. I don't know, it sounds so stupid."

"Not stupid." He shook his head. "Sometimes it doesn't seem rational or logical, but you're fighting fear—it's an invisible battle."

"But what am I afraid of?"

"What do you think?"

He'd asked me that same question the first day I met him—he'd asked if I was afraid of the threat of a blackout leading into the new millennium or the asteroid blowing us all into oblivion because that's all I would talk about. I'm not afraid of the dark, and I don't think oblivion would hurt so much if I knew I wasn't leaving everyone behind.

I think he knew this. I think he knew there was something else, something unsaid. I think it was why he kept asking me about my time capsule and why I write these letters. I think it was why he asked me to write one more.

"What about you, what are you afraid of?" I asked him.

His eyes were steady on mine, dark blue and growing darker, and there it was again, a shadow behind them that pulled the past forward and made him disappear for a moment to someplace I couldn't follow, someone I couldn't know. I opened my mouth to speak again—to tell him I was sorry, that I didn't mean it, that I would answer his question if only he would go back to the him before, the him I knew—but his eyes flicked to the clock on the bookcase.

"Time's up," he said softly.

By the time I packed up the pencils and gathered my things, he was already standing at the window, staring at the fields layered with frost, lost in a memory and weighed down with regret.

~ *Lia*

JANUARY 10, 2001

Dear Whoever You Are,

The preacher stood on the far corner of the intersection, waving hand-painted signs at cars coming off the exit ramp, his words coated in threats. His black hair was slicked back as usual, and he wore a pair of dark dress pants, a maroon scarf, and a tan overcoat that flapped open to reveal a white collared shirt underneath. A couple of cars honked at him, and he raised his voice—deep and thundering—and shook his sign for emphasis. I almost felt sorry for him, standing out there in the cold, echoing centuries of fear out of desperation for the world to believe with him.

"Good to know we're all going to Hell again," Josh said beside me, tapping his thumb against the steering wheel.

I tried to hide my smile behind my hand. It was the first thing he'd said the entire car ride home, and even though it wasn't much, at least it was something.

He was waiting for me at my locker after the final bell this afternoon, hands shoved in the pockets of his coat as he watched me approach from the other end of the hall. He asked me which books I needed for homework while I spun the combination on the lock, then reached over my head to grab them from the top shelf as soon as it was open. He took off before I'd even zipped up my backpack.

"Aren't we waiting for Mollie?" I asked, hurrying to catch up with him.

"Art project," he'd practically grunted.

Great. So it was just me and Mr. Good Mood today.

His strides were long and purposeful as we crossed the parking lot, and I strayed a few steps behind him while his friends pulled up in their truck, a thin layer of snow coating the hood. I raised my eyebrows at him, then walked on ahead to wait by the car. It was only a few seconds before he jogged over to unlock the doors.

We hit every red light on the way home. I could feel him hesitate as we approached the intersection off the highway—could tell by the way his foot hovered on the gas for a split second longer than it should have that he wanted to speed through, like he didn't want to be in the car with me any longer than he needed to. He looked at me out of the corner of his eye, then sighed and downshifted before stepping on the brake and rolling the car to a stop.

"What's with you today?" I finally asked, shifting in the seat to face him. The preacher's shouts were behind us now, his words like snowflakes melting on the ground, vanishing as quickly as they came.

Josh glanced at me—one, quick turn of the head before his eyes were back on the road. For a second, I wondered if he was going to ignore my words, too. But his fingers tightened around the wheel, and with a second glance my way, he sighed. "Sam's dropping out of school."

I wasn't expecting that.

"What do you mean he's dropping out? That doesn't make sense—he was just talking about transferring." I waited for him to say something else, but he kept his eyes trained ahead. "Come on," I said. "You can't leave it at that." His jaw clenched, and he pressed his foot on the gas. I stared at him in disbelief, my face growing hot with anger. "Josh! You have to tell me what's going on."

No matter how much I begged, he remained silent, his eyes fixed firmly on the road. I cursed him under my breath and crossed my arms and leaned against the window while houses whipped by in a blur of shapes and color, making them impossible to identify—

And there it was again, like on my birthday this past October, the night Josh walked us home—when, for a split-second, the world seemed to shift into something I didn't recognize, and I was lost on a street I'd wandered down a thousand times before. I reached my hand up to touch the window. The glass felt cold beneath my fingertips.

Cold and real.

I closed my eyes.

"Ask him," Josh said when he pulled up to my house minutes later.

I opened the door to the backseat and reached for my bag. He turned around, his eyes locking on mine like he wanted to say something more. Then he shifted his car into reverse, and I had just enough time to slam the door shut before he was backing out of the driveway, abandoning me with a secret I didn't want to keep.

*~ Lia*

**JANUARY 16, 2001**

Dear Whoever You Are,
    It's all my fault.
    "How is it your fault?"

I stared down at the notebook in my lap, the lined pages covered in Candy Apple roses and sloping suns that burned Yellow-Orange and the subtle scrawl of my name across Sky Blue. Exclamation points outlined in Pine Green, question marks tinged with Wildberry... Colored chaos of shapes and symbols turning the blank page into a work of—not art, but a tangle of scattered thought and avoidance.

"Lia? How is it your fault?" my doctor tried again.

I shrugged. "It just is."

Maybe if I hadn't begged Sam to take me driving yesterday after school—if I hadn't bribed him by offering to do his chores for a month—he wouldn't have a reason to be so mad at me. Maybe if I hadn't opened my mouth in the car—if I'd just driven us home like he wanted me to—he would've eventually changed his mind about wanting to quit school.

Maybe then everything that went wrong could have righted itself.

Maybe life could have gone back to the way it was.

Maybe...

"Why don't you start from the beginning," my doctor said.

We drove to the church parking lot at the edge of our neighborhood, empty except for a dented hatchback parked near the double doors. Sam wanted me to practice parallel parking, which would have been a lot more helpful if there were actual cars around, but I was delusional if I thought he would let me take the Camry on the road without a license.

His words. Not mine.

A half an hour later, his grip had loosened on the door handle and the words "Damn it, Lia" were coming out of his mouth only every third or fourth sentence.

"Okay, good," Sam had said, not bothering to hide the relief in his voice. "Let's go home."

But I didn't go home. Instead, I shifted into park and stared at the stained glass windows of the church in front of me as Sam asked me what the hell I was doing.

Then all hell broke loose.

"Why are you dropping out of school?" I asked him.

He grew silent. When I turned my head, he was leaning his arm against the car door, staring out the window at the wheat fields that surrounded the church and extended to the woods behind our neighborhood where we used to play, now just acres of dirt waiting for the first big snowfall of the year. I thought he would yell at me or curse out Josh for spilling his secret, but instead, he sighed and said college wasn't what he thought it would be in a voice so quiet, I had to lean over and shut the heat vents just to hear him.

You know when you're really close to someone, you can almost tell what they're thinking? Words don't matter because their expression says everything that needs to be said? I couldn't tell what Sam was thinking. Here was my brother who I'd grown up with—who lived down the hall from me my entire life, who shared memories and meals and eye rolls at Dad's lame jokes—yet we were nothing more than strangers now, occasionally passing each other in the world.

"He wouldn't even look at me when he told me he'd failed two of his classes," I told my doctor.

I tapped the colored pencil against the notebook in my lap, the faint trace of Purple Haze peppering a small section of the paper. Across from me, his arm rested on his desk (Dark Walnut), and his hand wrapped around the coffee mug (Golden Yellow). His eyes were steady on mine, waiting patiently for me to continue, and I mentally scanned all the shades of blue I could think of that might match their color (Navy, Cerulean, Aqua, Ocean), but nothing came close. They were the rainstorm, the cloud cover, the 3AM shadows chasing tiny flecks of light. There was something in those eyes no color could capture, a sadness not even a smile could tame.

"That must have been hard for Sam to admit," he said. "What did you say to him?"

I didn't know what to say. None of it was making any sense to me. Sam always got good grades in high school, so why should college be any different?

"Because college isn't high school, Lia," Sam said in the way he does when he thinks he knows so much more than me because he's four years older. "It's fine," he repeated. "I have a job at J&R lined up. It's fine."

I stared at him. Was he kidding? Was that what he really wanted? He had his whole life ahead of him, and he wanted to settle for some job at a manufacturing company? "But what about your dreams?"

"I don't have any dreams!" he erupted. "I just have this."

He got defensive then, calling me sanctimonious and saying what was so bad, anyway, about a good paying job with benefits and 401Ks and stock options and other things I don't care about or understand. I didn't get it. I didn't get it when Josh told me last week in the car, and I really didn't get it talking to Sam there in the church parking lot.

"How can someone throw their whole life away like that?" I asked my doctor. "How can you give up on something just because it's hard?"

"Sometimes you don't have a choice." His fingers curled around his coffee mug, then hesitated and withdrew. "Sometimes you have to give everything up if you want to start over."

But Sam never gave up on anything. He once stayed up all night creating a brand new diorama of Ancient Egypt after Bilbo chewed through the shoebox and ate the Sphinx. When he was a senior, he tore a muscle playing soccer and was back on the practice field three weeks later. And he's smart—really smart. He could be teaching or inventing or doing so much more than working on an assembly line.

I shouldn't have said that. It only made him madder. He said I didn't know anything about anything because I was too young to know what the real world was like, which is a crock of shit because I'm here, I'm living in the real world. I'm living, aren't I? I may not have my license or be on my own in college yet, but I'm still part of the world.

I tried to tell him this, but he just shook his head and yelled at me to get out of the car, and I yelled back that it was too cold to walk home. Then he started cursing at me and shouting that he wouldn't do that but to get out from behind the damn wheel and switch seats so he could drive us back, and I was so angry, I got in the backseat instead.

"You don't get it." Sam's voice was so quiet, I almost didn't hear him, but I sat up and watched him in the rearview mirror as we pulled onto our street. "College is just another reminder that I'll never be what everyone expects me to be."

He sounded so defeated, and for a minute, I could see him—really see him, the Sam he was back before we were all grown up and driving and talking about college. It was just me and my big brother in the backyard, fighting imaginary villains with sticks for swords, brother and sister taking a stand for the good in the world.

We pulled into the driveway where he paused, the engine still running, hand on the key. "Don't tell Mom and Dad," he said.

"It's funny how our lives are a lot like dominos," I said to my doctor, my fingertips running along the grooved lettering of the pencil in my hand. Gray—the center of light and dark, the essence of limbo.

The in-between.

"How's that?" he asked.

"It only takes one and we all go down."

*~ Lia*

## FEBRUARY 9, 2001

Dear Whoever You Are,

I was caught there again, trapped in a constant twilight like that fleeting moment at the beach where I dreamed I belonged to nothing and everything all at once, existing within a forever where I felt invincible, unshakeable.

But today...

I never want to imagine a forever like this.

At lunch, the cafeteria was filled with a million muted conversations—everyone was laughing and shouting, but they all seemed so distant, like I was observing another species from some faraway planet, listening to a symphony only they could hear. In French class, I stared at the test on my desk—at the mechanical pencil that lay beside it, willing myself to pick it up and start writing—but my mind was like quicksand clinging to foreign words, and it took every ounce of effort just to pull them out and write one sentence.

Everyone began zipping up their backpacks and walking towards the door in math class, but it didn't register that the final bell had rung until Mr. Moore set the chalk back in the tray and paused on his way to his desk.

"Amelia? Do you need help with something?"

I didn't know. I didn't know...

I shook my head and closed my textbook, but the faster I tried to move, the less my body wanted to listen. By the time I made it to my locker and outside to the school steps, half the building had already cleared out while the other half was making their way to practice or clubs or detention. The second wave of buses was already pulling away from the curb, horns honking and hands shooting out open windows as cars lined up to exit the parking lot. I scanned the crowd for Josh or Mollie, wondering if they were waiting for me in the car where it was warm, but when I looked across the lot, their space was empty.

*Wait for me!* I wanted to shout. I wanted to run down the steps after them and find them in the line of cars, but everything was moving in such slow motion, I thought if I tried to move, I'd be in slow motion, too.

A car horn drew my eyes down to the road. I watched Kelly Jacowski pull up to the curb and roll down her window. She was asking me if I needed a ride home, but her words seemed to reach my ears seconds after they were spoken. I wanted to say yes. I wanted to scream and wave my arms and yell, "Something's wrong with me, take me home!" But my brain wouldn't connect with my mouth no matter how hard I tried, and I could only stare at her like an idiot for so long before she got mad and said, "Fine, never mind" and sped off.

"You okay?"

The voice came from my right, and I closed my eyes and inhaled before willing myself to turn and look at him. Cory Bishop from my chemistry class was watching me, his warm, brown eyes narrowing as they settled on my own. He frowned and stepped closer, and I wondered how bad I looked, to see his face so full of concern like that.

"Lia..." His voice trailed off in a question.

*Something's wrong with me,* I thought.

I forced myself to focus on him, pouring all my energy into my next words. "Can you take me home?"

I don't know how I made it upstairs to my room. Probably one of those acts of superhuman strength that only seem to occur in dire circumstances. I could hear Izzy's muffled voice through the walls as she talked on the phone to one of her friends, and then the hum of the garage door closing and my mom calling to me from downstairs an hour later.

I didn't say anything. I couldn't. I could only lay on top of the covers on my bed, staring at the wooden dollhouse my dad had built for me when I was nine.

It has two floors and an attic—Izzy and I used to play with it for hours, rearranging the rooms into tiny apartments or hotel suites or pretending it was Cinderella's house before the ball. But that was years ago, before the furniture and dolls were packed away in plastic totes and stored in the furthest corner of my closet. Now, a pair of gym shorts and a bath towel were thrown across the roof—just another surface for stuff to accumulate.

I needed to take those clothes off the roof before my dad saw what I'd done—that's all I could think as I stared at the empty rooms. He'd spent the better part of a summer working on that dollhouse, and I didn't want him to think I didn't care about it because I did. I did, and I wanted him to know that. I wanted to get up and toss those dirty clothes in the hamper and pretend they were never there at all, covering something so special to me, but I couldn't will myself to move, even as Mom called my name.

She sounded faint and faraway, and the world felt so slow and out of sync that by the time I parted my lips, she was already standing in the room, telling me she was waiting to pick me up at school. "You said you were staying behind for *Typescript* today."

Oh. Right.

"I don't feel so good," I said. She was at my side in an instant, placing her palm against my forehead and sweeping the hair from my face. "I took my medicine like I was supposed to," I whispered. Even to my own ears, the words sounded hollow.

"What's she on?"

I heard Sam before I saw him, watching from the doorway with his hands tucked into the front pockets of his hoodie. Tears began to pool in the corners of my eyes, but I didn't have the strength to lift my hand and brush them away. I wanted to tell them I was fine—I just needed a nap so I didn't feel so tired—but no matter how loudly my mind shouted, the words wouldn't leave my mouth.

Sam leaned down near the end of the bed. I felt him take off my shoes and tickle the bottoms of my feet, but I barely flinched. I'm pretty sure they traded glances at that point. I'm pretty sure I don't want to know what they were thinking.

I don't know how I got downstairs any more than I know how I got upstairs. One minute, I was on the landing, and the next, I was staring at the cloth placemats stacked in the middle of the kitchen table while Mom opened a can and stuck something in the microwave, saying maybe all I needed was a little food. When she put the plate down in front of me, I could only stare at the green beans, watching the steam rise and evaporate into the air. My hand rested on the table, my fingertips grazing the cold steel of the fork.

"What's wrong with her?" Sam asked.

I didn't know. I didn't know. Someone help me, I didn't know. It was like my body was shutting down, and while my brain was screaming to just pick up the damn fork and eat a fucking green bean, it wasn't connecting to my hand. Like the wire had fizzled out. Like the link between my brain and my body had been broken.

"Can you say something?" my mom asked.

I barely had enough energy to part my lips. "Numb," was all I could mutter.

The rest is a blur. Sam says I would only respond in one-word answers, and when I began to stutter, Mom leapt into crisis mode by grabbing my jacket and helping me out to the car. I remember the fluorescent lights in the ER, remember laying on a gurney in the middle of the hallway because there weren't any rooms available, remember a doctor trying to get me to speak and tell him what I'd taken. I remember blinking back tears and the poke of an IV in the back of my hand. But it was like that was another reality, another Amelia, and I wasn't anywhere at all.

I started to feel better an hour later, like I was waking up and coming back into myself. By the time another hour had passed, my world was back to normal. The doctor said my drug test was clean, that it was probably just a bad reaction to the anxiety medication.

*No shit*, I wanted to yell, but I didn't. Not because I couldn't, but because I knew it was wasted energy when I already had little left. I just wanted to go home.

They discharged me with the recommendation that I talk to Dr. Denlinger about trying another medication, but I don't want to. I don't want to see Dr. Denlinger. I don't want to go on another medication. I don't want to feel numb like that ever again.

Because I know which one is worse now, and I'd rather feel everything a thousand times over than not feel anything at all.

~ *Lia*

## FEBRUARY 25, 2001

Dear Whoever You Are,

My mom was waiting for me at the kitchen table when I came downstairs this morning, a plate of buttered toast waiting in my usual place. I was still wearing my party dress, but I'd grabbed my hoodie off the doorknob on my way out of my room, and now I zipped it up and tugged at the hood strings as I watched Izzy slurp the rest of her cereal at the counter. My mom raised her eyebrows, and I sat in the chair across from her. We lingered in that silence until I reached for a piece of toast and went to the fridge for a glass of orange juice, trying to avoid saying what I didn't have the words for.

"You'll have to return Josh's coat," she said.

I froze. "That was Josh's?"

"He called to see how you were. So did Mollie."

My sister smirked. "Yeah, except she's pissed."

My mom scolded Izzy, telling her to hurry up and grab her coat, that Dad was waiting for her in the car. She dropped her bowl in the sink, and I winced as the front door slammed shut a second later.

I looked over at my mom. "Mollie's really mad?" I asked quietly.

Her eyes softened. "What happened, Lia?"

I don't know what happened—that's the problem. The details are still fuzzy, like the night was divided between the half I remember, where I gave Mollie her birthday gift and sat with the Engles and my parents for dinner and danced with my classmates, and the other half—where the world became a blur of intense light and deafening music and too-bright stars.

When Mollie called to invite me to her birthday party a few months ago, I couldn't keep the surprise from my voice or stop the wave of nostalgia that came after. I mean, of course I was invited—we've been best friends for forever, and our families have known each other for even longer than that. But there was a sincerity in the way she spoke, like maybe she missed me as much as I missed her, like maybe the distance between us was only in my imagination.

Like maybe our thread hadn't completely unraveled.

But then last night...

The party was held at the fire hall near the movie theater—the same fire hall that hosts an omelet breakfast fundraiser once a month and puts a sign out front reminding us to change the batteries in our smoke detectors each spring. Most of the kids from my class were there, loitering at the edge of the dance floor, and a few of the adults congregated in a corner by the dinner tables, sipping red wine out of clear, plastic cups.

I'd bought Mollie the set of paintbrushes I caught her eyeing the last time we were at the art store back in September and a "Sweet 16" charm for her bracelet. They were placed with the other presents in a corner of the room— next to the buffet lined with hot appetizers and chips and cheeses and a cake that was probably made by Dottie's Bakery downtown. Maybe I would have helped her and her mom pick out the decorations and the cake, like we did for her party at the roller rink when she was ten. But things were different now.

At least, they're not the same.

She was wearing a violet, knee-length dress with flowers bunched at the hip, and her hair was gathered in loose waves at her shoulders. She looked great. They all did—all the girls, like Bethany and Carly, who were surrounding her near the DJ's table. I wondered if they'd gone over to her house to get ready like we always imagined we'd do for school dances, even though it's been two years and we haven't been to a single one yet.

Not that it mattered. It's just that they were all wearing their hair in those waves, and Carly kept fiddling with the charm bracelet on her wrist that I knew was Mollie's because I recognized the horseshoe I gave her last year.

I got ready on my own—with a little help from Mom and Izzy. We went to the mall a few weeks ago, where Izzy helped me pick out a simple, black dress that dipped enough at the neckline to warrant my dad asking about the return policy. My hair was pinned back in a low twist instead of down in waves, but my mom let me borrow a pair of her earrings and helped me with my makeup.

I know that doesn't matter to you. I know you don't care what I wore, but I felt pretty. I don't know—I think something changes on the inside when you feel pretty on the outside. Like for one, brief minute it makes you believe that what you look like reflects who you are, and maybe that means something.

And it matters when other people seem to see that, too—like when Cory Bishop said hi to me as he was passing by with his swim team friends. He looked over his shoulder and smiled at me, and that one smile made all the difference between hello and, like, *hello*. All night we were two magnetic polls, constantly finding and aligning with each other—whenever I looked up, there he was, looking back. And then, as soon as Benji Harris and the other designers on the literary journal walked away, *there he was,* trying to hold back a smile and glancing down at the floor and back at me like he was the one who was nervous.

He asked me how I'd been feeling since...

Since?

Oh, right. Since he had to take me home after I'd gone practically catatonic thanks to my anxiety meds, barely saying two words the whole way because my body refused to cooperate with my brain. How was I doing? I was fine. There was no way in hell I was going to be anything but fine—especially not then, when he was standing in front of me, a full foot taller so that even when I stood from the table, I had to look up and he had to look down, and we were both entirely okay with that.

You have to understand something—Cory's one of the nice guys. He's one of those genuinely good people you know won't change just because he's on the swim team and breaking all sorts of school records, including Sam's. I've known him since the start of the sixth grade, when he moved to town and my class went on a field trip to some campground for a team-building exercise—where we had to help each other through an obstacle course by swinging on tires and navigating thin cables and balancing on logs. He's the kind of guy who isn't afraid to ask for your opinion on his history paper, who takes the time to say hi to you in the hallway and actually waits for a response, who holds your hand to make sure you get across the log without falling and then stays by your side for the rest of the course just because.

Standing there by the cluster of tables, it didn't feel like five years had passed since he first helped me find my balance and held my hand. It felt strange and surreal, but in a good way, like he'd always been there—first at the obstacle course, then on the steps of the school, and now among the pulsating music and party lights.

He told me he hadn't been able to talk to me since he drove me home. "What happened?" he asked. "Were you okay?"

I glanced at my shoes, at the floor littered with stray bits of crepe paper. "Bad day," I said.

I think he could tell I didn't want to talk about it because he just nodded and said, "Bad days are rough." Then he ducked his head and ran a hand over the nape of his neck and asked, "Today? Is today a bad day?" And I couldn't help but grin at his sincerity and shake my head and say, no. Today was turning out to be a good day.

He smiled at that—a smile that lit up his face and reached his eyes—and he nodded and told me he'd catch up with me later. He began to walk away, glancing back again as he crossed the room—

And I swear one of these days, I'm going to learn how to flirt and be endearing and confident and ask him to dance.

But I hate to dance, and I didn't want to dance, except maybe with him, and I don't know how to flirt or be endearing. I only know how to be me. The best thing is—he seemed okay with that. Because the only difference between seeing him tonight and passing him in the hallways at school or meeting him in the sixth grade when my jeans were caked with mud was we were at a party with music and dancing, and I finally felt pretty.

I want to remember that. I want to remember the two of us talking and flirting, if that's what flirting is. I want to remember him settling back into his corner with his friends, his eyes meeting mine over the top of a soda can, trying to hide a smile that I caught, anyway, and matched with one of my own. I want to remember tonight ending at that exact moment because I don't want to remember the rest.

Mollie pulled me onto the dance floor despite my protests, but no one cared that we couldn't dance. Bodies crowded into the space, and we moved and laughed and shouted to be heard above the roar of the music as multi-colored lights rotated around us until all I could hear was the steady thump of the bass, and all I could feel was the floor vibrating beneath my feet, and all I could see were flashes of red and blue and yellow light spinning wildly around me and catching me off-guard.

The smile faded from my lips. My hands dropped to my sides. The world seemed to slow down, even as my heart sped up—a measured wave shifting in time to a beat I couldn't hear. My eyes swept across the room, trying to find something familiar to hold onto, but all I could focus on were the sterno candles burning beneath the buffet trays, like that's what was making the room so warm, and the lights flashing in awkward patterns, like that's what was making everyone's faces so distorted, and the makeshift dance floor beneath my feet, like that's what was causing the room to tilt and turn and—

There it was again—that one thought ready to erupt like a volcano from the pit of my stomach, threatening to ruin everything and swallow me whole.

*Run.*

The music was too loud and the room was too warm and there were too many people, and I was too close to suffocating. And that word—a warning to find my way home, to the only safety I've ever known—repeating itself over and over in my mind until I couldn't catch my breath, like someone was sucking the air right out of my lungs. My chest heaved as I pushed my way to the edge of the dance floor. I tried to find my parents, but the crowd tightened around me until there wasn't enough air, and the room began to shift and sway.

Josh reached my side as I collapsed into a chair, my head bowed and eyes squeezed tight. He kept calling my name and asking me what was wrong, and why was I sweating and so pale, but his voice sounded so far away—the beat of the music becoming a drum that was too close—and I couldn't answer him.

Then there was my dad, taking my chin in his hand and forcing me to look at him. I think what he saw scared him because the next thing I knew, he was holding me up by the elbow and ushering me outside, and as soon as I was out the door, I was sucking in mouthfuls of cold air like there wasn't enough oxygen in the world.

He sat me on a low wall that lined a garden bed outside the building. A coat was thrown over my shoulders, and I pulled it closer around me and huddled against it, shivering even though my body felt like it was burning from the inside out. I heard my dad speaking to someone, his voice low and urgent, but I couldn't make sense of the words. I threw my head back and closed my eyes, struggling to ignore the ocean roar that filled my ears and the pounding that echoed in my chest.

The winter sky stretched before me when I opened my eyes again. Every star in the sky seemed to blaze with some kind of primordial comfort, and they were so bright and so close that if I reached my hand up, I knew I could touch them if I only tried.

I wanted to try. But the fire that burned inside me dissipated, and my breathing calmed and the ocean quieted, and I knew the stars were only an illusion—too far away to ever be held.

A palm was placed against my forehead, my cheek, and suddenly I felt so tiny and so sad at the loss of the stars, I started to cry. Dad kneeled down in front of me, his voice quiet and kind as he asked me what happened, what was wrong? I shook my head and held onto the lapel of his coat, sobbing and begging him to take me home.

My dad's footsteps faded into the distance as he crossed the parking lot. I watched him go, fresh tears stinging my eyes. I wanted to call him back, wanted him to stay, but someone else was there beside me, their hand resting on the back of my head, lips pressed against my hair. Fingers laced their way through my own in a source of comfort I've only ever known from him.

Josh's voice was calm and steady, a welcomed distraction from the beat of the music inside, still too loud, while I clung to him and stared up at the stars, still so close, until my dad drove up and they helped me into the car and we headed home.

"I'm sorry," I cried to Mollie on the phone this morning. "I'm so, so sorry."

I don't know what's happening to me, but I think there's something really wrong. I didn't mean to run out of her party. I didn't mean to leave my best friend behind. All I wanted to do was get some air because there wasn't enough air in there—in that room with all those people and the lights and the music, where I could only focus on running home. I knew I needed to stay, but I had to go because I couldn't breathe, and I was so scared because I felt small and helpless, and I could almost touch the stars.

It was nonsense and rambling, and the dial tone was the only response. The phone clattered to the kitchen counter, and hot tears spilled down my cheeks as I erupted in sobs.

"Oh, honey." My mom crossed the kitchen and pulled me against her, holding me without speaking.

There was nothing left for anyone to say.

*~ Lia*

## MARCH 6, 2001

Dear Whoever You Are,

I overheard someone at school once say that your taste buds change every seven years. If that's true, it makes me wonder how often other things change, too. Maybe the people you're friends with in elementary school aren't your friends by the time you get to high school. Maybe your friends in high school are replaced by the people you meet in college. Maybe those lifelong friendships you read about in books and see in the movies really are just works of fiction—a dream someone made up because they wanted it to be true, and the only place wishes come true are in books and dreams.

I'm still in high school, but I can already feel everything shifting and changing and morphing into something else, and it makes me wonder how anything ever lasts at all. Maybe forever is just a lie someone told once upon a time, and it sounded pretty and poetic and made us want to trust in something bigger than what our simple minds could imagine, and so we did. Except this whole time, it's been nothing but a joke, only no one is laughing—that's how much we want to believe in it.

I don't know if it's because of them or me or all of us—if it's something internal or if our friendship is just a byproduct of our environment and it's inevitable that as soon as we leave this town, we'll also be leaving each other behind—but it's already starting, that shift.

I'm not ready for it.

I want to keep believing in forever because I don't want to think that ten years of friendship is just wasted time or that memories don't matter.

My doctor frowned. "Memories matter, Lia."

He was sitting behind his desk again, and I was slouched in the hard, wooden armchair across from him. We were back to this—there were no colored pencils or notepads to sketch in today. Not this time. Not since I told him about my body shutting down thanks to the medication, and he spent half an hour after my appointment talking to my mom while I waited for them outside his office.

It was one of the few times I'd ever seen them speak, and when I followed my mom out to the parking lot, begging her to tell me what they'd said, she snapped that they didn't even mention me, so could I please stop talking for five seconds? I froze. My mom never shouted like that. Ever. Especially not at me. I was so surprised, my eyes began to burn with unwanted tears, but they disappeared quickly as I watched her get in the front seat, press the locks, and put her head on the wheel like she was the one who was about to cry.

I was still outside.

In the middle of February.

I pulled on the door handle and tapped on the window and opened my mouth to shout, but she unlocked the doors and started the engine, and I hopped in the passenger seat before she could change her mind. We didn't say anything the whole ride home.

"Memories matter," he said today. But the way the words sounded—like they were caught in their own past—I didn't think it was meant entirely for me. "Your friendship with Mollie matters. Time just changes things sometimes."

I didn't want time to change things. For so long, it was just me and Mollie, and I liked it that way. I liked that we had a friendship that felt like it would outlast everyone, and I liked that our families were friends because it meant we would always be connected to each other.

But now, everything's different.

I want to hang out in the art room with Mollie while Josh is at soccer practice because he's our ride home. I want to sit by the pool and cheer for Cory after he slips a note in my locker inviting me to his swim meet. I want to make some extra cash with Kelly by tutoring in the library, or listen to Bethany's little brother sing in the middle school talent show, or work on the literary magazine with Benji

Harris and be proud of the spring edition we distributed today. I want to do everything everyone expects of me—everything any normal sixteen year old can do—but I can't because I quit the magazine a month ago, and I take the bus home every day just so I can nap after school.

Insomnia isn't my problem anymore. Now, if I don't crash on the couch for at least an hour, I won't make it through dinner or be able to stay up and do my homework, and at the very least, I need to keep my grades up so I can get through this year and make it past summer.

But no one understands that. They see me sitting on my own in the back of the bus, resting my head against the cold window while they pass below me on the sidewalk, and they think that's what I want, like I have a choice, like I want our worlds to be worlds apart like this.

They see what they want to see. They don't see me.

Last weekend, Mollie and I tagged along with Josh and a couple of his friends to the pizza shop in the strip mall near the highway. The strip mall doesn't get a lot of traffic since Carvel moved out a few years ago—there's just a laundromat, the pizza shop, and a Blockbuster remaining. A couple of the stores have covered the windows in Kraft paper so we can't see inside, and the ones that don't are kept in darkness. If you lean your forehead against the glass and cup your hands around your eyes, you can see the skeletons of bare counters and empty racks inside, and the concrete above the store still bears the fingerprint from their sign telling anyone who cares to look what used to be there.

Kind of like these letters, in a way.

Mollie and I sipped our sodas out of plastic cups and sprinkled oregano over our pizza slices and glanced at Josh and his friends as they bellowed with laughter the next booth over. She and I used to spend summer afternoons riding our bikes in slow circles in that parking lot, talking about what life would be like when we got to high school and dreaming about our futures when we were thirty and old enough to have everything we could ever want. I dreamed about living somewhere exotic—like in a cottage in Bora Bora, surrounded by palm trees with a swimming pool two steps away from the house and the ocean five steps away from that.

The memory made me smile, and I reminded Mollie that she wanted a Winnebago once—completely decked out with a TV and phone in every room and a pool on the roof. She paused, cheese dangling midway between her mouth and the pizza in hand, then burst into laughter. The silence that had crafted a wall between us crumbled, and we spent the rest of the afternoon reminiscing about our dreams then and wondering what had become of them now.

When we're alone like that, it's easy to remember lost dreams. It's easy to feel like I know where I belong because I've always belonged right there, right next to her. But now, whenever we're at lunch or study hall or another one of Carly's Friday night parties, that's all forgotten again. All they seem to want to talk about is Mimi Liang's pink highlights or how Kelly made out with her boyfriend in the parking lot behind the empty ice cream shop, and it makes me wonder if I belong anywhere.

"I feel like I can't recognize them anymore," I told my doctor. "It's like they're half of who they used to be."

He chose his words slowly, carefully. He seemed to be doing that a lot more lately. "Sometimes people have a hard time separating who they were with who they want to be."

"That doesn't make any sense," I said.

There was a wish in his smile, like he didn't want his next words to be true for me, even if they were true for everyone else. "It will," he said.

"You sound like my mom."

"People grow up and grow apart," my mom had said when I told her I'd apologized to Mollie again at the pizza shop and how, even though we laughed at our memories and she says it's fine and that she understands, I can tell it isn't fine, and she doesn't understand. "That's just what happens. You'll survive this."

I know. I know I'll survive this. Everyone survives growing up. But this feels like something more. This feels like a part of my heart is being ripped out of my chest, and I don't know if I'll ever be able to catch my breath again.

Life can go on without Kelly and Bethany and Carly, but what about Mollie? What if this is only the start of something permanent, a deep fissure growing wider beneath the surface that's too late to be repaired. What if we can't ever go back? What if she's not my best friend anymore? Who am I without her?

No, really. Can you tell me?

Because I need to know.

~ Lia

## MARCH 11, 2001

Dear Whoever You Are,

Everything around me is falling apart, and I need you. I need you to tell me it's not up to me to keep it all together, even though I feel like it is, even though I want to. I need you to tell me everything will right itself again, that it'll all go back to the way it was before—for my parents, for my sister, for my brother who dropped out of college today, and now everyone is downstairs in the kitchen trying to figure this out without screaming at each other, their voices mixed with a fury and disappointment that's worse than any yelling.

I need you to tell me things don't fall apart for long.

Izzy's here, standing in the doorway of my room, clutching her art case like it's a shield protecting her from any residual outrage that might be aimed her way. For all I can tell, it is. "They kicked me out," she says.

"I know. I heard."

I don't have to tell her she's allowed in my room. It's one of those unspoken things that's always been and always will be. She sits on the floor and leans her back against the bed, opening her sketchbook to do her thing, much like I'm doing my thing, writing this letter. Only, it's not really a letter anymore, is it? It's more of a distraction—just a way to pretend we're not paying attention to the shouting match that's taking place downstairs. The door to my room is open, and every few minutes, we'll lean forward and strain to hear what's being said when their words become muffled again.

Mom and Dad want him to finish out the semester, but Sam keeps insisting he's failing, anyway, and he already has a job lined up. He just needs until the summer—then he'll find an apartment and pay them back for whatever wasn't covered under Mom's teaching benefits.

"He has it all planned out," Izzy says.

I nod as Mom's voice rises—"That's not the point, Sam!"—and glance over my sister's shoulder to see what she's drawing. It's nothing yet as far as I can tell—just a few stray lines reaching the corners of the page, just the charcoal beginnings of something brilliant.

"Think it'll be over soon?" she asks.

"I don't think so," I tell her honestly.

My mom is on the verge of tears. I can hear it in the crack in her voice, in the rise and fall of her words. It's funny how I can tell these things now, when I was oblivious back then—back in November when Izzy and Sammy and I sat in the doorways to our rooms, listening to our parents argue. Back when I never thought I'd hear her cry.

Maybe things get harder the older you get. It's easy when you're a kid: if you're sad, you cry. If you're angry, you yell. But then you grow up, and the world doesn't let it be that simple anymore. Suddenly, you have to hide the tears and pretend you're invulnerable. Maybe that's why adults yell so much in the first place—better to get angry than to cry. Better to yell than to show anyone you're hurting.

Except there's no pretending now.

Izzy's fingers are smudged black from the charcoal. She's holding onto it like she doesn't know what to do, staring down at the sketchpad in her lap, at the lines she's created there, too lost in her head and what's happening below us to pay any attention to her art. Sam's words are rushed as he pleads for my parents to listen to what he's saying, but my parents are having a hard time with that, so they start listing reasons why this is a really bad idea instead, and for a brief second, I understand him. And then again, I don't.

I don't understand this. Maybe that's why my heart aches like someone is squeezing every ounce of life from it, why I'm furiously scribbling in this notebook like I'm trying to race my tears with these words—because I understand him, but I don't understand this. I don't understand how a family, *my family*, can fall apart in a matter of moments, how everything can seem so perfect one minute—how we can eat dinner together every night and spend our summers in Iowa and attend each other's games and recitals and banquets—and then break apart the next.

None of our problems then were as big as they are now, and how does that happen? I need you to tell me how that happens. Is it because of us? Is it because of all of us—because we're not kids anymore? Does the older you get mean the more problems you have, making it harder for everyone to deal with them?

Are we causing this?

Please, tell me! Tell me something, tell me anything. Just…help me understand.

But you can't, can you? Because I don't even exist to you yet. Even if you read this—even if you're able to travel back in time and tell me how everything fixes itself in the end—maybe you can't. Because maybe you don't have the answers, either, even when you're all grown up.

I don't want to grow up. I don't want my family to yell and be split apart by one person's decision. I don't want everything I've ever known to change like it has—

Sam's on the stairs. I hear him curse under his breath, and I call out to him to come here for a second. He ignores me and wanders into his room to grab his keys, then pauses in my doorway.

"Not now, Lia," he sighs. His voice is thick with defeat.

Yes, now. I need to know what's happening. I need to know what Mom and Dad had to say. I need to know if he's really quitting school and moving out because what will happen to our family then?

"Leave it alone," he says. "It's none of your business."

"But it is my business. It's all of our business, and we can hear you shouting, anyway, so what were you saying?"

He shakes his head and says I'm too young to get it. His words are the same as that day in the church parking lot when he was teaching me to drive, the day I knocked the first domino down.

"I'm not some little kid." I glare at him and ask him how he can think I don't know anything about anything.

"Because you are some little kid. Both of you—you're just little kids."

Izzy rolls her eyes. "Both of you, shut up," she says, and stomps back to her room, leaving her art kit spilled across my carpet.

"I don't know what you want me to say, Lia." His voice is shaking, but I can't tell if it's from anger or something else. "I don't know what I want to do with my life, but it's not this." He exhales slowly, his eyes downcast like he's sorry for yelling. "Just... Go back to writing to whoever you're writing to." He gestures to the notebook in my lap, then turns and begins to walk away. "It'll all be fine."

I stare at him, wanting to say something, but the words won't come.

It's then that I realize he knows about these letters. It's how I know it won't all be fine.

~ *Lia*

**JUNE 9, 2001**

Dear Whoever You Are,

Sammy moved out today. I'm writing you this letter as I sit on the floor of his room, trying to imagine it as it used to be just a few weeks ago, before the boxes came and the furniture was moved and his trophies were packed away in storage bins and brought down to the basement for safe-keeping.

It's a different room now that it's empty. All that's left behind are some trash bags, an unplugged vacuum sitting in the corner, and a bunch of folded shirts he'd asked Mom to donate to Goodwill. Everything else has been bubble wrapped and boxed up and sent over to his new place—a one-bedroom apartment with a balcony overlooking a side street he'd found in a complex downtown.

It's not Sam's room anymore. Now, it's just four blue walls and a carpet. Just another room in a house where memories used to live.

Dad has spackled over the holes in the walls where Sam's pictures once hung so that now the blue is peppered with splotches of white, making the room look uneven and unsure of its fate. If I look up, I can still see pieces of tape adhered to the ceiling where his Smashing Pumpkins poster used to stretch above his bed. They missed that when they cleaned his room this afternoon. I don't want to tell them—the tape is like a reminder that Sam used to live here, and as long as it's still there, then it's like a piece of him still is, too.

Then again, maybe they already know. Maybe my parents saw it and ignored it because it's the last thing that links Sam's old room to this empty one.

Maybe not.

We helped him move this morning. His apartment is only fifteen minutes away and a few blocks down from the vet clinic, but the distance feels like the difference between the earth and the moon. That's what happens when you spend practically every day of your childhood across the hall from each other—when someone leaves, no matter where they go, it always seems impossibly far.

Dad, Sam, and Josh hoisted his bedroom set and a hideous couch he bought for fifty dollars at a garage sale up the stairwell to the second floor while Izzy and I carried the cushions and some of the lighter boxes. I don't know who had it easier—them with the heavy furniture or us with our thousand and one trips up and down the stairs. My mom cleaned the counters and the fridge and unpacked an old set of dishes that I'd bet any money was given to Sam as an unspoken peace-offering.

Still, my parents didn't say much the whole time they were there—just simple things, like "Where do you want the flatware" and "Watch out for the doorjamb."

As soon as we got back home, Dad got out the spackle, and Mom got out the vacuum, and I got ready to take a nap. They didn't say anything—no argument, no "Lia, come help us..." They only asked me to close the door so they wouldn't wake me, and then the soft scrape of the spackle knife slid against the wall in rhythm and the vacuum became a dull song. I squeezed my eyes shut and tried to imagine that Sam's room was still Sam's room.

At dinner, Izzy asked if she could move in there, now that Sam's moved out. I knew that was coming—his room is bigger and has its own phone jack, so of course she would want it. It's fine with me. I've spent sixteen years in my room. I don't want to replace any of those memories, even if it means trading it up for something better.

Mom and Dad exchanged glances and told her, no— they would figure out what to do with it some other time. I think there's a small part of them still holding out hope he'll come home, even though he's twenty and ready to be out on his own. I just don't think they thought it would happen like this.

Sam was just the beginning. Things won't be the same here anymore, and I don't think any of us are ready for it. Soon, I'll be going to college, and then Izzy, and then we'll all be on our own and what will be left? Just three empty rooms where we used to play and read stories and dream about who we'd be when we got older. But we're older now—at least, we're getting there. So where do all those dreams go when we're gone?

All these years sitting around the same kitchen table for dinner. All these years fighting over the remote control and mixing our clothes together in the laundry hamper and trading chores like some kids trade baseball cards. All these years walking out the same door to go to school each morning and walking back in when we finally come home at night. All of that's changed now. Because he's there, and we're here, and everything feels uneven. Like those splotches on the wall.

Dad will eventually repaint, and maybe it will even be a new color if they turn it into an office or a guest room—or if Izzy gets her way and is allowed to switch rooms. But no matter what, Sam is gone, and we can't go back to what we were before.

Outside, the sky's getting darker, shifting into a shade of blue that seems as unrecognizable as this room. From my place on the floor, I can see the tips of stray branches stirring against the window, and even though they don't seem to connect to anything, I know they have to connect to something.

I wonder if Sam's homesick. I wonder if he'll wake up tonight and be confused, trying to figure out why everything looks so different. I wonder what he'll think when he realizes he's not home anymore.

Then again, he's probably having friends over and ordering pizza and watching whatever baseball game is on TV. He's probably not even missing us.

Not like I'm missing him.

~ *Lia*

Dear Whoever You Are,

There were no fireworks at the Engles' tonight. Whatever was left over from last year remained tucked away in the box in their garage. And there was no Mollie. She and Benji Harris went to see the bands play at the park this year. I think it was supposed to be a date, even though they were meeting up with Carly, but she shrugged and was out the door before I could ask her anything else.

There weren't as many people at the barbecue this year, either. It was just my family and Sam, who drove over from his new place, and a few neighbors from down the block, sitting around one of those fire pits you can buy at the Home Depot and eating off reusable plastic plates—"Better for the environment," Mrs. Engle had said—while we listened to Justin string his guitar on the porch. Even Mr. Engle's burgers tasted different. I waited for my dad to say something—"What's your secret, Paul?" "Must be the grill"—but it never came. They just kept talking about the expansion of Dad's clinic, occasionally pressing down on the burgers with the back of the spatula, causing the flames to temporarily swell.

The age of traditions, it seemed, was over.

At eight, Mrs. Engle began putting plastic wrap on the food trays, and my mom came around with a garbage bag for the empty cups and used napkins while Mr. Engle drove Justin and Izzy to the park to meet their friends before the fireworks began.

"Coffee, Karen?"

My mom shook her head and said she and my dad were heading home. Then she turned to me. "You coming, Lia?"

No. I was fine there, slouched in a beach chair in front of the fire pit, listening to the soft hum of the boys' voices as they talked about soccer and Sam's apartment and who Josh's new roommate at college might be.

"I'll take her home," Josh said. He glanced at me, our eyes locking, and I remembered those same words being spoken late last year, when he walked me and Izzy home on my birthday.

*Why*, he'd asked then. Why had I been so afraid of the fireworks on the Fourth of July, he'd meant. I didn't have an answer for him then. I didn't know. Just like I didn't know why I was afraid now—a quieter fear that began to grow heavy in my heart the more they talked about whether or not Josh would get a place off campus next year and what kind of parties the frats liked to throw.

"Are you happy?" The question surprised me enough to look up. Josh was leaning forward in his chair, arms resting on his knees and drink in his hand, head turned towards Sam as he waited for an answer. "You know, that you dropped out of school?"

Sam shrugged and picked up a long, thick stick from the ground beside him, poking at the coals. The flames jumped and cracked, creating distorted shadows on their faces. "Happy enough."

I don't know if it was the firelight or his answer that changed him, but suddenly he wasn't Sammy anymore. Maybe he hadn't been for a while, and I just never noticed. The more I stared at him across the fire, the more I realized my big brother—the one who sat beside me on the bus my first day of school, the one who trapped spiders in cups and transferred them back outside because I didn't want to kill them, the one who cursed at me because I almost ruined his transmission when he was teaching me to drive—was now just Sam. Here he was, my big brother and someone new all rolled into one, and I don't know how I missed it.

But I did. I missed it. I missed him.

A few weeks ago, after he moved in, Sam invited us all over for dinner to check out his new place—now that he actually had his furniture rearranged and CDs unpacked and this really hideous picture of an 18ᵗʰ century noble that he "saved" from the dumpster hanging on his wall. I think my parents were actually impressed—not by the noble, I mean. My mom really hates that painting. But by the fact that he was already given a raise at his job and seemed proud of his apartment, and probably also because he cooked us a meal that included an actual vegetable. My dad and Sam went onto the balcony to talk for a long time after dinner while my mom and sister and I cleaned up, and when they came back inside, they were both smiling.

Listening to him describe his job to Josh tonight—the way he spoke and the light in his eyes that I don't think came only from the fire—I wondered if my parents saw that change in him before I did.

"You ready for school?" Sam asked.

I felt Josh hesitate before I even looked up. He glanced my way, his eyes meeting mine for a brief second before he cleared his throat and said he had almost everything packed. Then they were off—reminiscing about stealing a couch meant for the trash from Mr. Woodward's curb and dropping it off at a construction site; making fun of the time their friend, Andy, got his jeep stuck in two feet of mud, and it took half the soccer team an hour to get it out; laughing about memories they shared back then and knowing things would never be the same as this moment, tonight.

"You're being quiet."

It took me a second to realize the question was directed at me, and I dropped the hood cord on my jacket I'd been fiddling with and sat up straighter. "No, I'm not."

Josh chuckled. "Yeah, you are. What are you thinking in that head of yours?"

I was thinking everyone was vulnerable tonight, that this was the last summer. At least, the last summer before everything changed.

Things had been changing already. It probably started years ago when Sam graduated from high school. That was the beginning—things changed then. But time was speeding up now—now that Josh was going away and leaving everything behind.

Okay. Fine. Now that he was leaving me behind. Okay? I said it.

It doesn't matter, anyway. By the time you read this, it will already be done. He'll be gone—

And who knows where I'll be.

"You've got to lighten up, Lia," Sam said. I glared at him and asked him what the hell that was supposed to mean, but he just raised his hands in surrender and said he didn't mean it like that. "You stay in your head too much, you know? You lock people out."

"Yeah," Josh said quietly. "You even do that with me."

I paused and looked at him. Then I looked at Sam, who was leaning towards the fire, staring into the flames and poking pieces of coal with a stick. He raised his eyebrows but didn't disagree, didn't even look at me.

Let's go back to the remember whens, I wanted to say. I liked that better. Because at least when we were reminiscing, I could fall back into the past and take comfort in the fact that our families had a history, interweaving our childhoods together like a lace tapestry, spun out of delicate memories. At least then I could believe those strands spun on into infinity, instead of ending here.

But it wasn't ending here. At least, not in this moment. Josh and I stared at each other, silently wondering what we would say if we could write our secrets on the air tonight, until Sam slapped his hands on his knees and said, "Enough of that," and went into the house only to return minutes later with a jar of hot peppers, a package of hot dogs, and another bag of marshmallows.

Josh clapped his hands together and reached for the peppers, and Sam tore open the bag of marshmallows with his teeth, and I realized nothing was ending tonight.

*~ Lia*

**AUGUST 18, 2001**

Dear Whoever You Are,

We sat in his car in the empty parking lot overlooking the soccer field for what felt like hours before he finally spoke to me. In reality, it was probably more like five minutes, but time has a funny way of expanding or contracting according to how long you want something to last.

Third-period Economics? That's an eternity for ya.

Long goodbyes? Never long enough.

Outside, a morning rain was starting to fall, and he shifted in his seat and flipped on the windshield wipers. Their steady rhythm filled the silence as they rocked back and forth, clearing away tiny drops of water that blurred the world for moments at a time. I stared straight ahead at the thin film of dust that covered his dashboard, trying to ignore what lay ahead of us.

The trunk of his car was packed with a laundry hamper and boxes full of clothes and books, and a mini fridge pushed against the back of my seat as if fighting for more room.

*Get out of here,* I imagined it saying. *This car is taking him to another place, another life. You don't belong here anymore.*

*No shit,* I wanted to respond, and I almost did, if only to break the silence. I leaned forward to swipe my hand across his dashboard and clear the dust away, but he shifted again and cleared his throat, and I stopped and looked at him instead.

"What are you thinking?"

I wished he would stop asking me that. What was I thinking? Did he really want to know?

I was thinking maybe I should get back in my mom's car and drive to my house and toss that stupid turtle statue aside so I could dig up the lunchbox I had when I was seven and show him these letters. That's what I was thinking. I was thinking that, after two years of writing to you—some stranger I don't even know—and trying to understand life and why I feel so fucked up all the time, I still don't know shit about shit. He was the only constant variable in my life, the only thing that made any sense at all.

And now he was leaving.

All the crap you go through and all the lessons they teach you in school, and they never tell you how to say goodbye.

What was I thinking?

"I don't know," I lied.

"No, you do know."

I looked up because I didn't expect that. I should have expected that. Because he never knew when to leave me alone, and that was one of the reasons I needed him. But instead of telling him the truth, I told him I thought it was getting late, and he should probably get out on the road if he wanted to beat the morning traffic.

I regretted the words as soon as I said them, and I keep replaying that moment over and over in my head, wishing I could change it. But each time it's the same: the visible flinch, the short nod of his head, the way his eyes fell to the steering wheel.

"Okay," he said quietly.

He reached forward and started the ignition, and I stared at him, wanting to stop him, wanting that moment to freeze with us in his car, the parking lot lamp still burning in the pre-dawn, where it was just him and me and the changing tracks of his radio going on forever.

But I'm not naïve. I know you think I'm naïve, but I'm not. I know life doesn't work like that. It especially doesn't work like that.

"Okay," I said and grabbed my car keys off the dash. My hand hesitated on the door handle. I wanted him to reach for my hand like he did that night on the couch—remember that? That night when I couldn't sleep, and he just sat there and let me cry and held my hand until I fell asleep when I hadn't been able to sleep for weeks, and even then he stayed with me. I wanted him to tell me to wait, to tell me—

No. Now I'm just being stupid. Besides, wanting something doesn't do anyone any good, not now that he's gone, and it's too late.

I told him to drive safe, though other words hung on my lips, words I desperately tried to swallow down. His eyes locked on mine, and he nodded slowly. I opened the car door and stepped out into the rain and cold air—too cold for an August morning. He shifted his car into gear and backed out of the space, and I stood still for a minute, listening to the tires drive across the gravel and out of the parking lot.

He'd be back for Thanksgiving, he told me. We'd email and chat on Instant Messenger, and it wouldn't be so different—but it was. It is. And I don't get how people can't see that.

Sam made the same promise when he moved out, and I barely see him anymore because he's always at work or spending "quality time" with his new girlfriend. And Mollie and I wrote in each other's yearbook on the last day of school, vowing to hang out more this summer and reconnect, but we haven't hung out at all—and pausing to say hi for five minutes when she got home from the park on the Fourth of July doesn't count.

People say things won't change, but the minute they drive away in their car towards another life, they leave their old life behind. It's just true. It's just the way it works. And no amount of wishing can change that.

I think I knew that, watching him leave. But I don't think I wanted to believe it.

Because when I walked back to my mom's car and sank into the driver's seat and placed the key in the ignition, I didn't follow him. I just needed to stay there by myself for a while—just for a minute. I needed to wallow in a too-sad, Top 40 ballad in that empty parking lot as the rain began to let up, and the sun began to rise from behind me, and I cursed that the day couldn't give me just one minute of sympathy and flood the skies with clouds to despair in.

I sighed and shut the radio off and turned the wheel towards the exit, thinking maybe I could come back home and write this letter and then crawl under my covers and never get up. But a gray blur passed me as I drove across the parking lot, and I slowed and glanced in my rearview mirror as his car pulled to a stop a few yards behind me.

He opened his door and stepped out. I put my car in park and stared at him in the side view mirror, but he didn't move any further towards me, like the space between us was intentional.

"Why do you think that is?" he shouted, his voice deep and the words clear even through the closed window.

It was like that night he offered to walk me and Izzy home—that night that began in awkward silence and turned into a yelling match before he finally explained what was making him so upset. The night I turned sixteen—and he remembered—and I wrote my secret in glowing script that faded in the air as quickly as it appeared.

He was still there, still standing in the mirror. I shut off the engine and got out of the car, crossing the parking lot towards him until I was just a few feet away.

"Why do you think we'll never see each other again?" he asked. "That's the stupidest thing you've ever said."

Oh, was he keeping track? Because I was pretty sure I could come up with a few gems, myself.

Besides, I never said that—not in so many words. It just seemed like it was inevitable. I would be stuck here in this town for another two years, and he would be off at school leading a brand new life, and he would forget about me. We would see each other—because I'm pretty sure his mother would have a conniption if he missed out on our families' joint Thanksgiving dinner—but it wouldn't be the *same*.

I didn't know how to make him understand. Why didn't anyone understand?

He shook his head and crossed the space between us and reached out to touch my arm. I could feel the familiar warmth of his fingers resting on my sleeve even through my jacket. Then he was pulling me into a hug, his voice low and soft. "That's never gonna happen."

I buried my nose in the soft cotton of his hoodie and closed my eyes, wrapping my arms around his neck while he squeezed me closer.

Never say never.

*~ Lia*

## September 11, 2001

Dear Whoever You Are,
OK.
OK.
OK. I'm trying to write down what I'm feeling right now, but everything is so screwed up, and I don't know what to say. And I don't know how to say it without bursting into tears or screaming that our world is breaking, and my heart is breaking with it.

I'm sad. I'm more than sad—I've never felt this kind of sadness before. Not when my cat, Tempest, died, not when Grandpa Lawson died... Not ever. It's a kind of sadness I can't even describe, the kind that rips your insides out while leaving behind this one, small speck of hope that maybe, maybe...

And you don't know if you should keep holding onto that—if it's fair to let that hope sit there and get the chance to grow while the world falls apart, or if you should let it go before it rots because there are too many tears already, and things only seem to be getting worse as the day goes on.

"Did you hear?" I keep replaying Mollie's question in my head as the warning bell rang and she passed me in the hallway on my way to second-period math.

Did you hear?
Did you hear?
Did you?

But she was already moving through the crowd as the second bell echoed in the emptying hallway. When I got to class, my teacher was sitting at her computer, biting her nails while the rest of the students poured through the doors, grasping at whatever bits of information they could.

"There's nothing we can do," she said. "There's no more information." Then she stood and handed out a worksheet and told us to use the inverse to find the angle, like today was just a regular class, like today was just some regular day.

We believed her.

I think the world wanted to believe it, too.

But then we walked into Economics, where Mr. Murphey was standing in front of the TV, hand covering his mouth, and we watched with him in stunned silence, trying so hard to grasp the fact that, over two hundred miles away, people were facing this—this *thing*—this nightmare that went so far beyond any tragedy my mom ever told us about because it didn't seem real.

The footage they were showing over and over like the news anchors couldn't believe it themselves... It couldn't be real.

Then we watched the towers collapse.

Sam and Isabella were already there when I got home from school, and I dropped my bag beside the front door and hugged Izzy until she told me to knock it off. Sam was sitting on the edge of the coffee table, his face blank and remote in hand as he stared at the TV. I could see his jaw clench, and he kept raising a fist to his mouth, like he was holding something back. I sat down on the couch next to Bilbo and leaned against him, pressing my face against his fur, eyes trained on the TV. Reporters and experts and eyewitnesses weighed in, telling their stories, replaying the footage and the President's speech and repeating what they knew.

"I don't understand," I said.

"What's not to get, Lia, thousands of people are dead." Sam's voice shook with anger, but not at me. I thought I should be angry like him—that I should yell or be afraid or cry, but I didn't know how to do any of those things right then. I could only watch as the news stations pieced together timelines and tried to make sense of this change in the world that didn't make sense at all.

We sat together in the living room after dinner, two half-eaten pizzas growing cold on the kitchen counter behind us. Dad's eyes were red-rimmed, and I knew he'd been crying, or he wanted to cry, or maybe both. Mom's hand shook, clasped within my dad's, and we stared at them, waiting for whatever small piece of insight they could provide. But kid or adult, we were the same right then—we could think of a thousand questions and not one answer would be good enough.

My mom opened her mouth to speak, then immediately shut it again, like she didn't know what to say or how to say it. So we sat there in that silence until a small voice spoke up from the corner of the couch.

"The survivors, Mom..." Izzy said.

*Think of the survivors.*

My mom shook her head, a sob spilling out of her in an anguished wail I'd never heard from her before. This wasn't just crying. This was prayer and pain I've never felt, and I hoped to whatever god wanted to listen I never would. She covered her mouth with her hand, like that would catch her grief. Dad's hand moved in slow circles on her back, his head bowed, tears staining his shirt where they fell.

There's still people being pulled from the rubble as of the ten o'clock news, but they're saying to expect more casualties. No, not casualties. Casualties are what the news reports call them, but it makes it sound so cold and informal. Because casualty is what they say when they want you to feel sympathy during one segment and then become happy again during the next.

There is no next segment. There's just this.

I don't think anyone's going to forget this.

The thought that it was just a regular Tuesday morning makes me sick. I can't stop thinking how, right before, passengers on the plane were reading a book or closing their eyes for a nap or glancing out the window to see the skyline before they even knew what was happening. Office workers were making photocopies and pouring their first cup of coffee and getting ready for a meeting, and I was reading *The Great Gatsby* in class and trying to ignore Colby Donahue because he wouldn't stop talking, and no one saw it coming. No one knew. *No one knew.*

How does that happen? How can it be that one minute, you're planning for tomorrow, and the next, everything is gone? In the blink of an eye, you just cease to exist.

Maybe they felt no pain. Maybe they felt no fear. But the more I watch, the more I know that's bullshit because they had time—they had time to be in pain, and they had time to be afraid, and they had time to think about the people they loved before they looked out the window to see something fast and furious and—

nothing.

And it kills me.

No one saw it coming—not those people, and not their families, and not the goddamned preacher on the corner of I-81. You think you're okay, but then one day you'll be here, and the next day you won't, and life is still somehow supposed to move on. But how can it move on from this?

I think Mom has it wrong. Sometimes there are no survivors. Sometimes the wreckage goes beyond metal and concrete. Sometimes horrible people do horrible things, and it only takes a second.

But then again, maybe she's right. Because the newscasts are showing firefighters and police officers still working in the debris to rescue people who are trapped. And I think about how we were all so silent while we watched together in class today and how we sat in the living room tonight and rushed to my mom's side when she started to cry. It makes me think maybe there's still some good, even among the shit. Because if we're all feeling this…then maybe we're together in a different way.

I'm sorry. I shouldn't be writing all of this to you when I don't even know which is right and which is wrong anymore. By the time you read this, it will probably be so far into the future, the memory will have faded, and you'll be studying today like we studied Pearl Harbor or… I can't even bring myself to list anything else.

I don't know what to do with any of this. Time moves so quickly towards the next breath and the breath after that, and I could count all my breaths until the last, and it wouldn't matter because it would never be enough.

I'm scared, but I don't know what to be afraid of. I want to cry, but I feel so numb. I want to write things, scream things—I want to say so much to the world right now—but I don't know how, and it's going to sound stupid, but I don't know what else to do with it, and I need you to hear it with this breath because maybe it's my last:

I love you. I love you. I love you.

PART THREE

Dear Whoever You Are,

Sam's friend, Andy, said Mom's class was packed today. All of her students—even the ones who aren't on her roster this semester—wanted to hear what she had to say.

Except she didn't say anything.

She stood at the front of the crowded room, her hands on the lectern, and stared down at nothing—no textbook, no notecard, not a single piece of paper. She wouldn't even meet their eyes, even though they were waiting for her, expecting her to talk about it.

After a few minutes, she lifted her head, quietly said class was dismissed, and walked out the door.

~ *Lia*

SEPTEMBER 20, 2001

Dear Whoever You Are,

The preacher's gone. No one's seen him for weeks, and

now cars pass by that corner off the exit ramp like he was never there at all.

I just thought you should know.

~*Lia*

**OCTOBER 9, 2001**

Dear Whoever You Are,

There was a stray piece of white hair clinging to one of the small, ceramic pears that sat piled one on top of another in a plain wooden bowl on her desk. I stared at it the entire time she was talking, going on and on about how my panic attacks are triggered by fear—something about being away from my parents and how, now that I'm in high school, I have to start thinking about the future and leaving the nest, or some equally annoying metaphor for growing up.

*Please,* I wanted to say to her. My mom and dad dropped us off at my grandparents' farm in Iowa for a month each summer until I was eleven with a hug and a warning not to drown in the pond. I've been away from my parents before.

But she wasn't interested in anything I had to say, so I stopped listening, taking the time instead to glance around the office that should have been so familiar, but now seemed cold and unforgiving. A painting of a house stranded in the middle of a meadow hung on the far wall where his degrees used to be, and self-help titles replaced the fiction on his bookshelf, all alphabetized in an array of color that betrayed the ordered chaos he had once created there.

I sank lower in the wooden chair, leaning my elbow on the armrest and my head in my hand while she ranted about new worlds and vanishing security and letting go of the past because I was about to be a young adult, leaving childhood behind me.

It was such bullshit. I know enough to know that. Because you can't tell me life is really some separation between childhood and adulthood—like you flip a switch and suddenly everything you were before is gone. There isn't a before and after and then nothing in between—you grow up and then keep going. He taught me that.

I never got to thank him.

I shifted in my chair to glance behind me at the time, but her clock was sitting in a corner of the desk now, lacking numbers on its face and so yellowed by age, it might have been as old as her. It wasn't until I turned back that I saw it, half-hidden behind the window ledge and peeking out from behind the paisley-patterned couch.

The dark blue ashtray that once reminded me of the color of his eyes.

"Is he coming back?"

Her eyes grew wide and she straightened her shoulders, like I'd offended her by interrupting whatever speech she was still in the middle of. "He moved to New York to be with his family. I told you that already." Her tone was clipped, and for a second she reminded me of my Grandpa Lawson's second wife.

"But is he coming back?" I tried to hide the hope in my voice, but maybe she was smarter than she looked because her eyes softened and she shook her head.

"He wrote a letter his patients." I scooted to the edge of the chair and watched her open the top desk drawer, her manicured fingers flipping through half a dozen envelopes. "Ah, here you are," she said, reaching across the desk. "You can open it when we're finished."

Nope. I would open it right then and there, thank you very much. I slid my finger under the flap, tearing the seal, and pulled out the letter. My heart fell as I recognized the bold letterhead at the top of the page.

It was nice, as standard goodbyes go—just a few typed lines thanking his patients for the privilege of his confidentiality. He explained his reason for his hasty departure, wished us luck, and said we were in good hands with Dr. Pierce. I almost snorted because she was talking again, saying all sorts of things I didn't care to hear.

But then, at the bottom of the page, scribbled in blue ink, was a short message meant only for me:

*Keep writing your letters. Write when you're angry, write when you're sad, write when you're confused... Keep writing. There's a power in words, Lia, no matter how you say them. In a world where everyone is screaming to be heard, sometimes it's the whispers we need to listen to closely.*

"Well?"

I hastily rubbed the back of my hand across my eyes and looked up. Dr. Pierce was peering at me through her glasses—making her eyes look wider than any eyes naturally should be—and I felt my cheeks begin to grow hot. There wasn't any patience in her voice like I expected from someone like her. Just, "Well?" Like it was my Grandma Lawson scolding me the day I knocked over her milk glass vase, asking, "What do you have to say for yourself, missy?"

I folded the letter and sat back, staring at those pears on her desk. Suddenly, I was noticing everything about them—the flecks of gold in the paint and the light film of dust that layered the rim of the bowl and the sun that streamed through the window and reflected off the ceramic, merging the gold and the green and the light so it reminded me of a fairy tale.

She leaned forward, tapping her pencil against the edge of the desk. Well? It asked in rhythm. And that single piece of white hair, ruining the perfection of the pears and the light and the fairy tale I wanted to believe in.

"Tell me what you think," she demanded.

I think we're finished here.

~ *Lia*

# OCTOBER 26, 2001

Dear Whoever You Are,

There are some memories that are burned in your mind— moments you relive over and over again because they're good and you want to remember them, or they're bad and you can't forget them, or something was so unpredictable that it accidentally left an irreversible imprint on your life.

I'm starting to think those are the moments that end up changing you.

Remember when I got a "D" on my history test when I was a freshman? I can still hear the squeak of Mrs. Hadley's orthopedics against the tile floor as she walked by our desks, handing back our graded tests at the beginning of class. I'd taken mine with an eager smile, expecting to see an "A" at the top of the paper. But there it was, that big, red "D," circled and starred and highlighted with exclamation points all over the page—only, not really—and when I looked up, Mrs. Hadley raised her eyebrows, saying everything I didn't want to hear in just one look.

That was it. That was all it took. The longer I stared at my answers, trying to figure out what went wrong, the more tears began to well in my eyes until they threatened to spill over and stain the paper. That's what's so upsetting—not the thing itself, but the unexpected.

Like when you're walking past the school and out of nowhere you trip over some tree roots that have funneled through the cracks in the sidewalk. It's like the earth is trying to remind you it has always existed and will continue to exist no matter how much concrete you pour over it to try to cover it up. But you ignore that because this is a civilized society with modern conveniences like pavement, and that arrogance causes you to trip and fall and skin your hands in some kind of twisted version of instant karma.

And then... Then, you're so stunned that you actually tripped and fell, like you haven't been walking your entire life, your face grows hot and your vision blurs, and you wish the earth would just open up and swallow you whole.

Not like that happened to me. I mean, I'm just saying... It's kind of like that.

What I'm getting at is the unexpected happens, and that's what shakes you up: the falling, not the fall. Every single time.

Which is why I expected to cry when the planes hit the buildings and the towers collapsed and my mom fell apart. But I didn't. And I still haven't. One month since the world's been grieving, and I can't grieve with it.

I don't know what's wrong with me.

I can cry when Mollie forgets my birthday. I can cry when Bilbo eats something he shouldn't and Dad has to keep him overnight at his clinic. I can cry when Josh makes promises that we'll talk and then we don't for a month because he always has his away message on, and his Instant Messenger profile is set to some obscure Emerson quote that I'm pretty sure he heard in his Intro to Philosophy class.

And I can cry when I fall, when I kneel there on the pavement and stare at my bloody hands, absorbing the stinging pain until I'm ready to get back up and wash the dirt away because falls happen. They just do.

But I can't cry when I'm in line at the grocery store and there's another magazine cover of someone suspended in air ninety floors up, frozen in a photograph like what came before and what happened next don't exist. I can't cry when the newspaper comes in the mornings with another headline above the fold highlighting how everyone is afraid to open their mail because we don't know what we'll be breathing in. I can't cry when I turn on the TV and they're replaying footage I still see even if I close my eyes, and I watch the towers crumble again and again and again.

I can't cry. I'm supposed to be crying—it's what normal people do when horrible things happen. Not when life trips you up and you get your answers wrong and you have to say goodbye to someone you know you'll see again... You cry at this—at the stuff that means something.

So what's wrong with me?

I don't make any sense. It's the only explanation. I don't make sense. *Nothing* makes sense. And no matter what I read or how much I think about it or how many times I replay that day over and over in my mind, it's like there's this big question mark that's haunting me. None of my friends get it—they don't understand why I still want to talk about it, and I don't understand why they don't.

I got fed up with them today. As soon as they started talking about some concert that's coming to the convention center next month, I stood and grabbed my lunch and wandered across the cafeteria to the faculty lunch table, where I told Mrs. Giudieri it's been a month and I still haven't cried. She smiled this sad, knowing smile, and the teachers scooted their chairs closer to each other to make room for me. I sat there and picked at the chips on my tray, listening to Mr. Murphey explain the political and economic complications of a world that won't be the same again.

Which was great and all, but that's not what I needed.

I needed to know how Amelia Garrett and her brother could board the Titanic expecting to make it to America, only to be trapped on a lifeboat waiting to be rescued and watching people drown in freezing waters. I needed to know how Samuel Breck could come to Philadelphia expecting to become a merchant and go about his business, only to watch everyone in the city suffer from a violent, incurable illness. I needed to know how Isabella Breen could set off with her family in a covered wagon expecting to arrive in California, only to watch the people around them starve and die from hypothermia.

I needed to know how to expect the unexpected.

I need an answer. Not even a full answer—just a piece of one, just a fragment of understanding so I can figure out why I feel like half a human and how to become whole again.

I need to know if the passengers boarded their flights expecting to go to California. I need to know if the people in those buildings took the elevators to their offices expecting to talk over coffee in the breakroom, to type important memos to their colleagues before lunch, to answer phone calls and sign paperwork and go home in time to meet their kids for dinner. I need to know if they had plans and dreams. I need to know if they thought they had time.

I need to know if they felt trapped or alone or abandoned, if they knew nobody was coming to save them—

And if that's why they jumped.

"They knew they couldn't stay."

Mrs. Hadley's voice was soft, her words purposeful and vulnerable all at once. Even among the noise of the crowded cafeteria behind us, we could hear her, and we sat in silence, recognizing the impossible choice and that this was our life now—purposeful and vulnerable, all at once. Beneath her glasses, her eyes were red and rimmed with unshed tears. She looked at me and nodded.

That's all it took.

Now I'm crying like I'm still falling.

And I don't know if I'll ever stop.

~ *Lia*

Dear Friend,

We're friends, right? I know I don't know you, but I can talk to you, and after all this time, maybe you know me. Maybe that's the first half of friendship—finding someone, anyone, you can be honest with.

I wish he was still here. I wish I could see him and talk to him so I could answer his question—that question he'd asked me the first day in his office, an earnestness reflecting in his eyes that made me want to trust him immediately, even if I didn't want to say the words out loud.

*What are you afraid of?*

There's something happening to me. It started with the insomnia and continued with the panic attacks, and now I don't know where it will end. I'm scared. And I wish I could tell him that—finally, honestly.

The pain started a few months ago—short bursts of electricity running up my spine and through my shoulders like static shock. It was there and gone so quickly, I thought I'd imagined it, so I never said anything. Maybe no one would have believed me, anyway.

The aches followed, pushing deep into my thighs and beyond the muscle, like I'd just run a thousand miles, my legs becoming so weak I could collapse under the weight of myself and nothing—not ice packs or heating pads or massages—would ease it.

Dr. Denlinger checked my temperature and had me inhale and exhale as he listened to my lungs and asked if I was getting enough exercise—

"Because you've gained some weight, you know."

I know. He really didn't need to remind me every time I saw him.

"Her eating habits haven't changed," my mom spoke up from her chair in the corner.

Dr. Denlinger frowned and pursed his thin lips together like he was doubting even her. "Could be a virus," he concluded. "That would account for the fatigue. Or it could be growing pains."

Growing pains. I liked the sound of that—because it couldn't be more true. Growing up hurts more than anything else.

It hurts when someone takes a piece of your heart with them to college, then ignores your typed hellos and unspoken "I miss you." It hurts when you call your best friend, only to find out she's out with her other best friends, and you keep expecting to hear from her and never do. It hurts when you're too young to hang out with your older brother and his friends at his apartment, and you and your little sister are too old to play with your dollhouse the way you used to, and instead you're stuck in this limbo on a Friday night with nothing to do but write letters to strangers and wish that growing up didn't have to hurt so much.

When I look around the cafeteria at school, I see everyone talking about their grades and who's dating who and how cool some concert was, and all I want to talk about is how we've reached this age where we're supposed to know who we are and how I feel like the closer I get to defining myself, the further away I feel from that person.

The further away I feel from everything.

I'm just this blob floating in the water, just a—what's that thing that floats in the water for boats to see? A buoy.

That's right. That's what I feel like. A buoy drifting out to sea while all these boats pass me by without so much as a second glance. I'm here for them. I exist for them. But they don't even notice me. I'm so ordinary, I've become invisible.

I want to talk to someone about growing up, but this… This doesn't feel like regular growing up stuff.

Not when your body aches right down to the bone and you're so tired, you have to put your head down at lunch. Not when your history teacher calls on you twice before you realize your hand is raised and you're so confused, you can't remember the answer to a question you've known all your life.

And not when you're fainting in the locker room before gym class, sinking into the narrow space between the lockers and the bench before you realize what's happening.

That's what happened today—what finally led to this latest visit to Dr. Denlinger. I fainted in the locker room before gym class. Blacked out, passed out, whatever you want to call it. It's the second time it's happened since summer, only the first time I was in the shower, and my mom thought I'd gotten overheated because I like the water scalding.

This time wasn't like that. Not even close.

The other girls were already dressed in their uniforms and pulling their hair into ponytails by the time I got my shirt on because I was so stiff, I could barely move my arms.

"I can wait, if you want," Mollie said, but the whistle had already blown inside the gym, and I didn't want her to get in trouble when I still had to put my sneakers on.

They filed out the door until the locker room was silent and I was alone—and grateful for it. Because I could take my time and not have to hide the constant pain that ran the length of my body, spreading through my arms and legs.

But being alone meant no one was there to catch me when I fell.

I don't know what happened. One minute, I was standing in the middle of the locker bank with one sneaker on my foot and the other in my hand, and the next minute, my head felt so heavy, I couldn't hold it up anymore. There was nothing else around me, no other sound—just my own breathing, deep and steady, and then… Nothing.

My knees buckled beneath me, and I felt myself falling in slow motion as the world blinked away. It lasted only a second, but it was long enough so that when my vision cleared, I found myself underneath the wooden bench, my sneaker on the ground beside me, the taste of blood in my mouth.

Everything after that is a blur. I kept hearing my own shallow breaths like an amplified echo in my ears. Tears spilled out of me, but I didn't realize I was crying until I reached up and felt the collar of my shirt was damp.

Mollie said I walked out of the locker room wearing a sneaker on one foot and just a sock on the other, my fingers weaved through the laces on my gym shoe like I would never let it go. She said everyone stopped running their laps as soon as they saw me, and Mrs. Bryce rushed over and started asking questions that I answered in single-syllable words. But it's all so fuzzy, and the memory only becomes clear when someone tells me what happened.

Everything was out of focus. Sentences were spoken and questions were asked once, twice, three times before I remembered to respond, but my voice seemed to belong to someone else, like I was too far away and couldn't find my way back.

Nothing was real.

Not the stiff paper towel pressed against my lip, or Mollie's hand on my arm as she guided me out of the gym to the nurse's office, or the stares and teases and shouts from classmates as they poured out of their classrooms when the bell rang. My body was just a body, and I was completely disconnected from it. It was like I was floating down the halls, wearing my gym uniform and half a pair of sneakers, and everything around me was just an illusion we were passing through.

Mrs. Dietrich helped me lie down while she tried to call my mom and dad, and suddenly I felt like I was six years old all over again, except I was too big to fit into a makeshift bed of armchairs and blankets anymore. I think I knew then, lying on that vinyl cot in the nurse's office, that popsicles and cartoons and a few days tucked in bed couldn't fix this. It showed in her eyes, but Mrs. Dietrich didn't coo as she wiped the blood from my lip and took my temperature. She said she'd call me later, but Mollie didn't stay after she dropped off my backpack and clothes and left to go to her next class.

I was too old for sympathies now.

I changed my clothes. I tied my shoes. I went to my locker to get the books I would need for homework tonight. Then I signed myself out and waited on a bench in the courtyard for someone to pick me up and take me home.

The worst part of growing pains is that, at some point, you realize you actually have to grow up.

~ *Lia*

NOVEMBER 9, 2001

Dear Whoever You Are,

I thought I wanted to travel the world and be famous once—the famous Lia Lenelli. It has a nice ring to it, doesn't it?

But I take it back. I take it all back.

Because right now the world is too big and so loud that I feel like I'm just another moving part on this big machine that makes it all go 'round and 'round, and I'm getting lost in the mechanics and not remembering that I'm still just a girl. Amelia Garrett Lenelli. I'm still somebody.

Aren't I?

~ *Lia*

NOVEMBER 22, 2001

Dear Whoever You Are,

I wish my Grandpa Lawson was still alive so you could meet him. I know that doesn't make a whole lot of sense, considering the fact that by the time you read this, it'll be so far into the future, I might not be alive, either. But I wish you could. I think you'd like him.

We used to go to his house in the city for Thanksgiving dinner every year until he and his second wife moved to Florida. That's when they started flying up for Christmas, and he'd spend three days teaching us how to play card games or helping Mom roll the dough for sugar cookies or carving wooden tulips out of scrap wood using Dad's workbench in the garage. I'd bundle up in my winter coat and sit on the metal stool next to him, listening to old music on a crackly radio as I watched him coat the flat petals in vibrant blues or reds or yellows. When they were dry, he'd pick up the smallest paintbrush and create intricate scenes on each flower—ships on a raging sea, a Ferris wheel at a carnival, a windmill in the middle of a tulip field.

The morning before he went back home, he stood in the entryway, suitcases beside him, and handed one to each of us. He told us he was building us a bouquet, like it was his promise to us that we'd see him again next Christmas, and every Christmas after that.

I have nine of them sitting on a shelf above my bed.

My mom got the call the week before Thanksgiving that year. I heard the phone ring, then my parents' muffled voices through their bedroom door. I slept with my head at the foot of the bed that night, just so I could see the silhouettes of my flowers in the dark. The next day, we piled into the minivan and drove down to Florida for the funeral. I helped my dad sort through papers—putting receipts in one pile and anything that looked important in another—while Sam took Izzy to the boardwalk and Mom made funeral arrangements.

He was buried at the top of a hill beside his wife, who'd died a year earlier. We never went to her funeral. I barely knew anything about her, except for some insane reason she insisted on baking oatmeal raisin cookies whenever we visited. I don't think she knew what to do with kids—she'd never had any of her own, and Mom was already grown up by the time Grandpa remarried—so baking was probably a pretty safe bet. I never thought to ask my mom about her. It never mattered until now, and my mom never talked about her except for after the funeral, when we stood on the hill next to their burial plots.

"She was the one he couldn't live without." Her voice was faint and without rhythm, like the priest who had recited psalms over my grandpa's casket earlier that hour.

We were staring at the sliver of ocean that peeked between concrete blocks of condos. Behind us, Dad walked through the maze of headstones with Izzy, who was busy pointing out names and dates and reading everyone's epitaph out loud, and Sam was eyeing two men in blue coveralls who were leaning impatiently on their shovels a few feet away. The air was beginning to grow thick with humidity, and all I wanted to do was get out of the dress I was wearing and into my bathing suit and run into that small strand of ocean water that seemed so close but was miles away.

But Mom was still standing there, her gaze steady and unflinching. "There's an ancient myth that says the gods granted two lovers their wish to die within an hour of each other so they didn't have to be apart for long," she finally said. "Then they were turned into a tree. Or a bush, or maybe a twig—I can't remember."

Metal had begun to scrape against dirt behind us. I could hear my dad, already halfway down the hill with Izzy, calling for us to meet them at the car.

"Their bones were twisted into roots."

I blinked against the sunlight. "I didn't need to know that, Mom."

When we finally got home, it was the day before Thanksgiving. Mom flipped out before we'd even walked through the door, yelling about how she didn't have a turkey, and though we told her we didn't care—that we could just order a pizza from the place near Carvel—she insisted on having a real Thanksgiving dinner. I mentioned it to Mollie that night, who told her mom, who invited us over, and that was the start of it: Thanksgiving dinner with the Engles.

Sometimes I think it was Grandpa Lawson who brought us all together, in some weird, preternatural way. Like maybe he knew how much we would be missing him, like maybe he knew we needed our best friends. I don't know. Maybe that's just me wanting it to mean something then, just like I want it to mean something now.

Because I want to believe that we can live in our own apartments and go to school in new cities and be friends with different people and still feel like home to each other. I want it to feel like no time has passed since we last saw each other—our lives becoming so entwined that we can always pick up right where we left off, like Grandpa picking up that paintbrush year after year. I want there to be a reason we all come back together, even though our lives feel like we're an eternity apart.

Sam brought his new girlfriend to dinner this year. Mollie spent an hour on the phone with Benji Harris. And Josh…

With Mollie on the phone in my room and everyone else downstairs watching football and carving the turkey, I retreated to Izzy's room because it seemed like it was the last true sanctuary, the one place that wouldn't change—at least, not for another couple of years. Her artwork is pinned up with thumbtacks on every inch of wall space—ethereal watercolors featuring gardens and temples and forgotten grottos overrun by tropical flowers. I realized then that watching her paint was like watching Grandpa Lawson— the same concentration, the same smooth flick of the wrist.

Izzy has her tulips scattered on her bookshelf. I was looking at them when Josh came in. He stood in the door-way, hands in his pockets, asking me what I was doing and how have I been. He was wearing a shirt that matched the color of his eyes, but I couldn't look him in the eye. I didn't want to.

Instead, I picked one of the tulips off the shelf—the last one Grandpa Lawson ever made for Izzy. It was painted a dark purple, but otherwise completely blank—no design or scene like all the others he'd created over the years. Just a purple tulip. Just a regular flower. I didn't get it then. I still don't get it now, but I figured it was something special, something he was saying only to her. Now it was speaking to me because that's how I felt—like I could have been special once, a canvas to fill with another dream, but now I was simply forgotten and empty and always waiting for what wouldn't come.

Only, I didn't say that to him. Instead, I told him about my Grandpa Lawson because Josh would have liked him, too.

I showed him the rest of Izzy's tulips. He studied them, holding them in his hands like they were something sacred, until Mollie came out of my room, paused and glanced at the two of us, then asked if I wanted to watch a movie later, "Like old times." I began to follow her down the hallway, thinking maybe Grandpa Lawson really was bringing us all together again, when I heard Josh call my name behind me, his voice soft and uncertain.

"I'm sorry, Lia," he said. "I'm so sorry. I thought I'd go to school and things would be different. And that you—that I—" He paused and ducked his head, and I stared at him. I'd never seen him this nervous before, not even on my birthday on that October night—the night he stole the sparklers and maybe something else. When he raised his eyes to look at me again, there it was—the same something I couldn't name then, reflecting the hallway light now, only this time, I wondered if it wasn't in my eyes, too. "Sam told me how bad it's been. I'm sorry."

I shook my head. "It's fine."

It was the only thing I could say. Because it had to be fine. It had to be fine because I couldn't bear to think it could be otherwise.

I couldn't blame him—it wasn't his fault he went away to college and I was stuck here because I'm two years younger. It wasn't his fault he was living his life, too busy for me. That was just the natural order of things and nothing could change it, and I needed to accept it. It was just the way it was, the way it would be from now on—I'd always be this one, small thread linking him to his life here, and he'd forget me as soon as he was gone again because the world is huge, and he's a part of it now. And there are a thousand more people for him to meet who are prettier and smarter and healthier, so why wouldn't he forget all about me? I'm nothing more than a part of his past, just a girl who once thought she could be a part of his future, now vanishing into nothing, and it's fine. It's fine. It has to be fine.

Oh, God. It's not fine.

I couldn't breathe. I wanted the earth to open up and swallow me whole—and why does that never happen? I wanted to go back to where we were months ago; I wanted to fast forward past this. I wanted too much again.

I turned to go downstairs, but he reached out, his fingertips resting on my arm, telling me to wait like I'd wanted him to do the morning we said goodbye. "I swear I'm going to be here, Lia. I swear it. Because I—" His voice caught, and he cleared his throat. "There are some people you'll do anything for, you know?"

My heart pounded in my chest, heat creeping into my cheeks. He was so close, I could feel the warmth of his breath, and I imagined I could hear the words that have been lingering between us all this time in his next exhale.

"Hey, you two. Dinner's ready," my dad called up the stairs.

Josh pulled away.

He sat beside me at dinner, and when it was time to say the blessing that we somehow only seem to say at holidays, he laced his fingers through mine. We stayed like that while dishes were passed and Sam's girlfriend was welcomed until he finally let go and reached for the basket of rolls.

The last tulip my grandpa painted for me was of a bridge. Just one, single stone bridge that tapered off into nowhere. I remember I was disappointed at the time—I'd expected intricate scenes of cascading waterfalls or a beach dotted with colorful umbrellas, and the one, lone image confused me. But he just winked with both eyes, a knowing smile hidden inside them like a secret I've yet to decipher. It's still up there on my shelf above my bed, the last of the nine.

And my favorite.

*~ Lia*

**FEBRUARY 18, 2002**

Dear Whoever You Are,

I don't belong to their stories anymore.

At lunch, my friends talk about their play rehearsals or the cute guy they saw at the music store or what happened at Carly's house last Friday night, and I open my eyes and lift my head from where it was resting on the table because I want to know what happened, too.

But I can't. Because I wasn't there, and I've grown tired of asking. Their world is going on without me, and I can't do anything but sit back and watch, and honestly? I don't know if I want to be a part of it, anyway.

Sometimes I wish they would ask what's wrong with me. Sometimes I want to tell them I don't know, that I've been to half a dozen specialists in the past three months and they don't know, and this not knowing is terrifying, but thanks for asking because it means something that you care.

I've started eating lunch with Mrs. Giudieri and Mrs. Hadley. I'll hang out for a little while with my friends so we can pretend everything's normal, but then they'll start talking about preparing for the SATs and choosing their senior projects and whether or not their boyfriends want to go to the junior prom, and all I can think about is which doctor I'll be seeing next. I just want to be able to tell someone I'm scared, but I can't because we're in the high school cafeteria, and no one wants to talk about that kind of stuff here.

So I'll spend the last ten minutes of my lunch period with Mrs. G. and Mrs. Hadley while they talk about teaching or writing or history. And they're so passionate about what they're saying—which surprises me because I didn't think Mrs. Hadley was passionate about anything—it makes me think that someday I might be able to find something like that, if only I could think about something other than this.

Sometimes I'll chime in on their conversations, and for those ten minutes, I feel like I matter—like my thoughts and ideas mean something. They don't look at me funny when my mind goes blank mid-sentence and I forget what point I wanted to make, or when I have to ask Mrs. Hadley to repeat herself three times because the words coming out of her mouth seem like a foreign language. They simply ask me if I'm okay, and I can't believe how much that matters—to simply be asked if you're okay.

I wish I could shake myself out of it, like this whole thing is just a mess of mind over matter, but no matter how hard I try to convince myself I'm fine, I know I'm not. My body feels like it belongs to someone my Grandma Lenelli's age when I'm not even old enough to vote yet. My head hurts all the time, I can never find my balance, and I can't seem to get warm even though I'm wearing two shirts and a sweater and I'm sweating all the time.

All I want to do is sleep, and in some twist of irony, that's all I can do these days—like my insomnia is a thing of the past, and now I have to live through the other extreme. I'm barely getting by with a C-average in all of my classes—even Creative Writing, which I'm sure is disappointing Mrs. Giudieri—because every time I look at my notebook, the words seem alien, even though I wrote them. I have to re-read each sentence five times before my brain clicks on, and even then I have to struggle to make sense of what it was I was trying to say.

These letters—writing to you, whoever you are—have become my only salvation.

I'm scared to think even this won't last.

Anhedonic. That's a good word, isn't it? I learned it from Dr. Denlinger today. Anhedonia. It sounds like a melody or an Italian phrase that belongs in an ancient opera. It means you can't feel happy about the things you used to enjoy—empty, unmotivated, uncaring.

In other words, Dr. Denlinger said, you're depressed.

No shit.

But it was the way he said it—like that was the solution to all my problems rather than a symptom of something greater. I can tell you why I'm depressed—it's because life is going on out there while I'm still stuck in here, in a doctor's office. Every normal teenager is planning for the future and going on dates and to dances, and I'm afraid to leave the house because what if I pass out again in school or when I'm shopping or hell, even in my own driveway on the way to the car? My friends are setting goals and thinking about what they want to do when they graduate from college, and I just want to make it through high school and see eighteen.

He didn't want to hear that. He didn't want to hear anything I had to say. Because I'm too young to know better, right? I'm too young to know what's going on in my own body, too young to have my own suspicions about what might be wrong—I can't possibly believe there's something more serious going on here.

I'm just making it all up.

I stared at Dr. Denlinger from my place on the exam table. He stared at my chart in his hands.

"Repeat that, please?" My dad stepped closer to him, and my mom lay her hand on his arm, her head tilted like maybe she'd heard wrong, too.

I didn't. I heard him loud and clear.

Dr. Denlinger sighed, set the chart down on the counter behind him, and crossed his arms. "We see this all the time," he said. "Kids are naturally suggestive—they'll believe what they want to believe. Sometimes it's to get out of school or for the attention or—"

My dad pointed to the door. That's it—no words, just the pointing. His face was getting redder by the second, his fist clenched like he was holding himself back for the sake of everyone in the room. I started to cry as soon as the door clicked shut behind them, hot tears spilling down my cheeks. My mom stroked my hair and shushed me like I was two years old, but I didn't mind, didn't try to pull away. I felt like I was two again—tired and afraid and needing my dad to defend me. She pressed her cheek against the top of my head as I leaned against her, whispering in my ear that the doctor doesn't know me, and they know I'm not like that—and he doesn't. And I'm not.

But maybe I am. Maybe he's right because he's the doctor, and he sees this all the time. Maybe I'm making it all up for some subconsciously twisted reason I can't even begin to figure out. Maybe I really am imagining everything—because it feels like my legs are on fire, but they look perfectly normal without so much as a rash. And the tingling in my hands and feet is probably just them falling asleep because I always sit with my legs tucked beneath me. And the classical music I hear coming from the far corner of my room at night must be because someone left the TV on, or one of my neighbors is blasting some symphony so loud I can hear it from across the yard because that's crazy. No one really hears music that doesn't exist like that. That's just another figment of my imagination—an opus I'm remembering from some music class long ago that's looping back through my memory.

I wish my doctor was still here. I wish he'd never moved to New York. I wish that was his office I was sitting in, even if it had to be in that uncomfortable wooden chair, passing colored pencils back and forth as he listened to me—really listened to me the way only one other person ever has. He'd lean back in his chair and place his elbows on the armrests, his mouth pulled down, though he wouldn't be frowning, and his eyes would grow darker with some kind of knowledge that I don't think came only from his books. Then he'd ask me questions and actually wait to hear the answer.

I need someone like him here to tell me it will get better. Because I'm starting to wonder if it ever will.

I wish I could go away to someplace foreign like Argentina or Portugal or Alaska—anywhere but right here, right now. I want to get away from the kids at school who look at me like I'm a stranger, even though I've known them since we were all in diapers, and a doctor who thinks...

I don't even know what he thinks, but I'm pretty sure it's nothing good. It makes me so mad because all I've ever tried to be is good, and what does it matter because here I am, feeling like I'm dying, anyway.

Except that's not possible, is it? I can't go anywhere because I'm only seventeen and we can't afford it, and besides, the world doesn't allow for it, anyway. It doesn't care that you feel like you're drowning—when all you want is to be a part of something again, to have your very existence mean something more than it does in this moment. It doesn't care that you're a good kid—that you've always been a good kid—any more than it cares where you come from or what you've done, so long as you can prove who you are right now. The world doesn't care because life's not fair, and I get that. But you know what? It should be. Life should be fair.

Because the world is better than this...isn't it?

Maybe that's why I started writing these letters in the first place. Maybe that's why I'm still here, three years later, whispering to you when the rest of the world is shouting. Because these aren't just letters, they're wishes.

I wish people listened to each other the way my doctor listened to me. I wish we could see each other for what's real instead of what we seem. I wish we could get the chance to explore that for ourselves because I'm starting to think we're all caught in the in-between of who we want to be and who everyone else wants us to be, and there's not enough time to discover who we actually are.

I wish that when you open my time capsule a hundred years from now, the world is kinder. I wish it's better. I hope I played some part in that.

I don't know. Maybe it doesn't make a difference because I'm just one person. I can't change anything on my own—hell, I can't even get Dr. Denlinger to listen to me, never mind have a say in anything important. It's not like my voice counts and, even if it did, someone else is always speaking for me. Like these doctors who think they know what's best for me by ignoring me.

Maybe that's why I started writing, too. Because for the first time in my life, no one is speaking or thinking for me. I can finally be heard.

Even if you're the only one that's listening.

*~ Lia*

## MARCH 30, 2002

Dear Whoever You Are,

Did I ever tell you about our summers in Iowa?

There's nothing there—it's just acres upon acres of farmland peppered with the occasional small town that boasts a bank, a diner, and a church or synagogue (or both, if you're really lucky). We have to drive an hour to get to the nearest movie theater and a half an hour beyond that to find any chain restaurants and strip malls. That's okay, though. We have all those things here. The whole point of spending our summer vacation in Iowa was to get away from that. At least, that's what I can make of it now, looking back.

Back then, Friday nights at the movies were a special occasion—one that required us to wear sundresses or collared shirts and shoes that weren't sneakers. We'd go to an early showing of whatever family film was playing, then to dinner—walking five blocks for ice cream cones with Grandma afterwards while Grandpa Lenelli followed us in the car in case we got tired. Izzy always fell asleep on the ride back to the house, but I tried to stay awake for as long as I could. There was something magical about those car rides—like leaving a place sprinkled with crowds and lights and watching it grow more and more distant the farther into the country we went made the night seem like the fading entrails of a beautiful dream.

We spent a full month on the farm while my mom taught summer classes and my dad went back to work at the clinic. I wonder if growing up in Iowa had something to do with his love of animals because whenever they joined us for that last week, it was like I could see the kid in him—the way his face lit up and he relaxed.

Maybe that's just what going home does to you. Maybe it brings some piece of your past self to the surface.

We'd stopped going for the full summer break by the time I turned fourteen—mostly because Sam had his soccer and Izzy had camp, and I didn't know how to be anything but an ungrateful brat who complained about the weather instead of feeling nostalgic for feeding the calves and riding on the tractor with Grandpa and those Friday night drives.

When I think about it, I wish I could reverse time and just be happy with helping my Grandma gather the eggs to sell at the farmer's market near the one and only gas station in town instead of running out to swim in the pond or getting annoyed at the chickens. Because I was happy then. I was just too stubborn to recognize it.

It's kind of sad how that works.

Mollie came with us that year. Everything felt different, but not just because she was there—other things made it different, too. The pond had grown algae, and Grandpa and Uncle Jim had taken away the dock—it was just lying there in the overgrown grass a few feet from the water like it didn't know what to do. The dairy cow I'd named Iris when I was eight had been sold to another farm down the road, and there was barbed wire around the perimeter of the field instead of the split rail fence that Sam and I used to climb over to get to the horses on the neighbors' farm.

Maybe I was different, too, because Mollie and I spent the week lounging on the front porch reading magazines and listening to my CD player instead of giggling about getting our boots suctioned to the mud and hunting for four-leaf clovers in the field. And when it rained, we stayed inside to watch music videos on MTV like we were actually having fun.

I don't know. Maybe we were. Maybe that's what fun is when you're about to go to high school and you're stuck on a farm for five days. I just wish things had been different. I wish I could have shown her the tree where the robin fell out of its nest and we nursed it back to health, or how to hold the bottle for the calves at feeding time, or even my Grandma's stand at the farmer's market because she sells the best apple butter.

Maybe if I had done all of that and things were different then, they could be different now...

We're not friends anymore. She doesn't believe me. She thinks I'm "doing this" to get sympathy, to get people to like me, to get out of school. I don't even know the reason. But she couldn't be more wrong.

I don't have any friends left. Josh and I instant message each other all the time, but he's not here, and Cory's dating Kelly Jacowski, and Bethany's so busy with student council and the spring musical I barely see her even when I am in school—which, I'm trying, but I'm so tired and my body hurts so badly and feels so weak, it's hard to even move.

My mom keeps telling me to hang in there—that I'm a survivor like my namesake—and growing up, that was nice and all. But my namesake survived the sinking of a ship that was deemed unsinkable and here I am, sinking into oblivion, wasting away from one day to the next.

I'm not her. I'm not that Amelia Garrett. I'm just Lia...

And barely even that.

I don't remember who I am. I don't mean that in the same way I forget that butter goes on the toast, not in your orange juice or that dirty laundry goes in the washer first, not the dryer, but in a way that I don't recognize myself anymore. I don't know who I am—not because I'm still in the process of figuring it out but because everything that seemed to make me *me* has been stripped away—

And I've become nothing instead of something. There's nothing left of me.

Sometimes I wish we could still spend our summers in Iowa. Maybe that would be enough to remember who I am and turn me back into who I was, like it used to do for my dad. But my grandparents handed the farm down to my Uncle Jim last year and moved into a retirement community.

There's no going back.

Maybe some people do survive the sinking of unsinkable ships.

And some people don't.

~ *Lia*

## OCEANS IN IOWA
### A Short Story

*by Amelia Lenelli*

I wonder who would come to my funeral if I died today. I wonder who would cry if I shuffled my sneakers to the edge of this ridge and followed the crumbling dirt down to the boulders below. Nothing would save me—there wouldn't be a tree limb to get caught on or bales of hay to land on or an ocean current to sweep me away like in those stories.

There are no oceans in Iowa.

It would be just me and the rocks and one short step towards oblivion.

Does oblivion hurt? If you concentrate hard enough on the feel of the wind threading its way through your hair, blinding you with wild strands of brown that match the ground you left behind, do you begin to believe it will carry you, cradle you, all the way to safety?

Do you remember that the fall always ends, that in a moment you'll meet ground again? Do your eyes remain open? Or do they unwillingly shut in a last, desperate attempt to block out the inevitable. Does the storybook of a dissatisfied life flicker through your thoughts, or do you only see the permanent picture of the ground sixty feet below you. Does regret come too late? Does abandon come too soon?

I wonder what they'll say when they find my car parked a hundred yards away, the engine cool but the keys still in the ignition. I wonder if anyone will notice the missing keychain—the one she gave me on my sixteenth birthday—or if they'll realize it's gone when they see the silver key ring around my finger and turn my hand over to find it clutched tightly within the shelter of a fist. I wonder if it will leave an imprint on my palm when they uncurl my fingers, if they'll notice it's only half a heart, the other end of "friend."

I wonder if they'll make this bluff a shrine to me, if they'll light candles and say a prayer so my soul can get to God-knows-where. I wonder if they'll erect one of those white Christian crosses that you always see along the highway, with a flower tied with twine around the base, and if they'll religiously replace the flowers surrounding it on each anniversary and birthday.

Maybe classmates will bring teddy bears and candles and hold each other for support while their parents lament that I was "too young, much too young" before clinging to their sons and daughters with shaking hands and relieved embraces. Maybe teachers will gaze upon my grinning photograph—a tribute to healthier times—their lips lined in a grim expression as they mutter, "She had such a bright future ahead of her," and neighbors will nod their heads in agreement as they reminisce on my days as a child, tracing pictures with colored chalk on the dark pavement of my driveway, dressed in a pink flowered sundress and matching Jellies sandals.

She'll probably come on her own, after the crowds scatter to get on with their evening activities—dinner still to be made, children still to be bathed. She'll kneel in front of the flowers and candles and stuffed animals and photographs, not even caring that her brand new designer jeans are becoming soiled. Her tears will drip down her face and splash to the ground, creating her own Iowa ocean.

She'll struggle with her thoughts. Unable to form words, she won't speak. Her right hand will open, and dangling from her finger will spill the other half of my heart—jagged, split. She'll place it in front of my smiling picture, fresh tears blurring blue-eyed vision, and her other hand will gather grains of earth and lightly, lightly bury what was once there.

I wonder when their memories of me will fade, when they'll stop coming to pay their respects. Friends will hug at graduation and go their separate ways to colleges where they can see real oceans and live real lives. Neighbors will set out For Sale signs and pack their lives into U-Hauls before driving off, forgetting the little girl who used to wave every afternoon as she hopped off the school bus, plastic lunchbox in hand. Maybe my family will move, too, ready to start fresh where the memories aren't so suffocating.

She'll come every few months for the first few years to throw fresh flowers she'd purchased at the gas station over the bluff, turning away before she can see them land. Then the flowers will stop falling, and she'll stop coming.

The teddy bears and candles and smiling pictures in silver frames will be cleared away by contractors wanting to develop on that land—"the perfect view," they'll say. And no one who lived there for years will protest and exclaim that the site is sacred—a memorial, a memory.

The machines will come and erase all traces of me, a mechanical tide in an Iowa sea.

**APRIL 3, 2002**

Dear Whoever You Are,

My parents are scared. I can see it in their eyes when they ask me if I think I can make it to school today, and I shake my head no because I don't even have enough energy to lift my hand and turn off the alarm clock. I can feel it when they pause in my doorway before they head to work, when they tell me they love me and they'll check in at lunch, but I'm so tired I can't bring myself to say those words back, even though my mind is screaming them.

When Josh calls every night, the words are always there on the surface, but I can only listen quietly while he tells me about his classes or his friends or some party the soccer team is throwing at the end of the semester. His voice is alive and comforting, and I keep quiet because I love listening to him talk. For those few minutes, I feel like a normal person—like I can still be the Lia he drove to school every day, the Lia he stayed up with all night, the

Lia he sat with before the world was awake on the day we said our longest goodbye.

I'm part of the world again when I'm with him, and I can't change that. I don't want to change that. So, when he asks me how I'm feeling, I tell him today was a good day. I showered. I got dressed. I made it out the door.

I don't tell him that I only imagined myself feeding Bilbo and making breakfast and packing lunch, that I only imagined driving myself to school to take tests and finish projects and contribute in discussions about T.S. Eliot's *The Waste Land* like I want to.

I don't tell him that I make it to the front door, hand on the doorknob, trying to push myself to do what, rationally, any healthy person should be able to do. I don't tell him that I never make it any further than the front walk.

I tell him, *it's okay, I can do this.*

I don't tell him that I can't.

But I think Sam does. Because it's like he already knows. I hear it in the tone of his voice, in the hesitation in his words before he hangs up, like he wants to say something more.

"Hang in there, Lia," he says instead. Always, *hang in there.*

*For how much longer?* I want to ask. I stare at the cordless phone in my hand, now silent from his absence. I swallow the words back down.

I can't tell my mom or dad or Josh that I'm scared. But I can tell you, can't I? I can tell you anything. I can tell you how life feels like nothing more than an illusion—like my mind is fighting with itself trying to distinguish reality from the dream when everything seems like it's passing in a haze. I can tell you that mornings are the worst—when time seems to slow down and the cobwebs get that much thicker, like I'm in the middle of waking from a long sleep, though I've been awake the whole time. I can tell you that evenings are better, but even then there's that reminder that something is happening to me because the world is asleep and I'm awake and wondering how many more days this can go on.

Hang on, everyone keeps saying. But hang onto what?

I watched my mom make dinner from my place on the couch tonight. She thought I was resting and listening to the TV, but instead I was watching her rinse the chicken legs beneath a spray of water in the sink before rolling them in bread crumbs and plopping them into a baking dish. She was making my favorite comfort meal. She didn't ask if I needed it—it was like she just knew.

Izzy was seated at the kitchen counter, her school books spread out like she was conquering the kitchen. She was reading from her worksheet, comparing each question to last night's homework and complaining that it was the same, only worded differently, and how was it fair that they had to do the same homework twice? My mom raised an eyebrow as she placed the baking dish in the oven and set the timer on the microwave, but she let my sister continue.

In another life, I would have agreed with Izzy. I would have said something smart and annoying, like telling her to write down "see previous answer" on her homework. She probably would have listened to me, too.

But that was before, not now. That's how it is these days—life is split into before I was sick and after, and now all I can do is agree in my head because it takes too much energy to speak the words out loud.

My mom caught me watching her. She smiled and asked if I needed anything. I shook my head and struggled to stand.

"What are you doing, I'll come to you," she said.

But I needed to move. I needed to feel like I was doing something more than just decaying on a couch.

It took me a while to get to the kitchen. I held onto the back of the couch, the doorframe, the walls for support as I shuffled my way in because I couldn't conjure enough energy to lift my feet half an inch off the ground. Izzy silently slid the stool out next to her, but I shook my head and collapsed into a chair at the kitchen table instead. Stools were too tall; stools were out.

"You have an appointment with Dr. Denlinger tomorrow," my mom reminded me.

"Why, so he can tell me it's just another virus?" I asked. I immediately regretted it. My mom was trying, I know she was. And I wasn't helping anything by being a sarcastic brat.

But she didn't seem to mind. In fact, I think she agreed with me. We were all at a loss as to where to go next. A few weeks ago, we went to see a neurologist at one of the top teaching hospitals in the country. It took us four hours to get there, and after stumbling twice during a balance test, he sent me for an MRI of my brain.

"Anything in there?" my dad joked at the follow-up last week.

The doctor laughed, then patted my knee. "She's fine. A little deficient in vitamin B, but that's nothing some supplements can't fix."

I cried the whole way home.

"I don't get it," Mollie said when I told her. "Do you actually *want* to be sick?"

Of course I don't want to be sick. But I *am* sick. That's the thing—I don't want to be, but I am, and no one can figure out why. What I want is someone who can connect the dots so this can all be over and I can get better. I want to get better. But I'm only getting worse. That's the problem—why is that so hard for people to understand?

Izzy was silent at the kitchen counter, staring at her worksheet, though I could tell she was listening. My mom sat down at the table next to me and took my hand.

"We'll figure this out," she said, smoothing my hair away from my face. "You're a survivor."

I shook my head as hot tears began to spill down my cheeks. Because I'm not. I'm not a survivor. But how do I tell her that? How do I say to the one person who believes in our ability to endure—the one person who believes the most in me—that I'm not going to survive this? How do I admit that when I'm lying down and my legs are aching so badly—like every muscle is being squeezed by one of those vice clamps on my dad's workbench—all I can do is cry and beg for some relief, no matter what that looks like? How do I tell my mom that I'm beginning to accept it, because I'm fading away anyway, and maybe it's easier this way. Because I'm only seventeen years old—I haven't really lived yet to begin with. Maybe it's easier when you're young because you don't know what you're missing.

So now I can spend the rest of my time here knowing that it's been a really good life so far and prepare myself for whatever comes next. Because something has to come next, doesn't it? This can't be it, this can't be the end. There has to be something more—another life, a different place—something beyond this. There has to be.

This can't be everything there is.

Please tell me this isn't everything there is.

"Oh, Lia."

Don't tell me to hang in there anymore because I have nothing left to hang onto. Prayers don't work and miracles don't matter, and I'm not any more special than the next person. Why should I think I deserve to live any longer than anyone else? What makes me different? What makes everyone think I'm going to survive this—whatever it is. Maybe I'm not. Didn't anyone ever think of that? Maybe I'm not a survivor after all.

"Don't you dare say that," Mom said, her voice rising in anger.

"But I'm not!" I shouted, a cry stuck in my throat. "You named us after all these survivors like you think we're the same—you named us Amelia and Samuel and Isabella like we're them—but we're not them, Mom. We're not the same."

They survived, but maybe we won't. Maybe I won't. Because everyone is saying I'm fine when I'm broken, and there's nothing they can do for me when I'm pleading with them to fix me, and maybe that's just how it goes.

"I'm sorry," I cried. "Because I want to stay. I want to stay, but I don't know how."

Everyone says the survivors are the lucky ones because they didn't die, but who's to say that being left behind is any better? When you're left behind, you have time to fear what you escaped—that final inevitability. You can spend your whole life looking ahead at what's to come, questioning if there's anything beyond this, fearing that there might be nothing after all.

We're not the lucky ones. None of us are. Maybe none of us are survivors in the first place—not when we're all dying, anyway. No one really survives in the end.

So maybe this is just me, and this is my life, and this is how that story comes to a close.

My mom went silent. I could hear Izzy sniffling at the counter. I took a deep breath and wiped away the last of my tears. "I don't want to fight anymore," I said. "I don't have anything left."

Her eyes were fixed on me, her voice unwavering. "Then I'll fight for you."

I know you can't hear me, but won't you help me? Because I don't want this to end. I don't want my story to be over.

I don't want to jump.

*~ Lia*

**APRIL 4, 2002**

Dear Whoever You Are,

She knocked on my bedroom door like she actually expected me to be asleep—a soft rap with her knuckles that I wouldn't have heard if I was. The light from the hallway spilled into the room as she opened the door wider. Bilbo lifted his head and blinked before huffing his protest and nuzzling his nose into his hind legs. When the door began to close again, I mumbled against the pillow and reached for the lamp on the nightstand. Bilbo groaned and yawned and jumped down from his place at the end of the bed, running downstairs to curl up on the couch or Dad's armchair or wherever he would least likely be disturbed.

My mom stepped into the room and closed the door behind her. "Did you fall asleep okay?"

I nodded and scooted over for her to sit on the bed beside me. Falling asleep wasn't the problem—it never was anymore. But it was like my sleep cycles were all messed up because as soon as the numbers on the clock hit three, I was awake like I'd never even been asleep at all.

"She needs to stop sleeping during the day," Dr. Denlinger had said during our visit today. "That's why she's waking up at night."

Which would seem to make sense, so I can't really blame him for that logic, except I keep telling him I'm so tired, so why can't he do something about that?

We were armed with a list of symptoms and possible diagnoses written on a piece of notebook paper the last time we saw him. When he walked into the room and I showed it to him, he glanced over it briefly before asking me where it came from. I could tell it took all of his restraint not to roll his eyes when he handed the list back to me.

"You can't diagnose yourself based on what you read on the internet," he said.

"Why not? You don't seem to be doing such a bang-up job." The words flew out of my mouth before I could stop them, but between you and me, I didn't really care. My mom sighed and raised her eyes to the ceiling. My dad hid a smile behind his hand.

Dr. Denlinger was pissed. He ripped the sheet of paper out of my hands and went down the list one by one:

"No lesions on the brain, so you don't have Multiple Sclerosis. Lyme Disease is rare and you tested negative. Your thyroid tests came back in the normal range. You're too young to have arthritis."

"What about the chronic fatigue one?" my mom asked.

"I don't believe in Chronic Fatigue Syndrome," he said. "There's not enough evidence to support it. My *professional opinion*—" he emphasized those last words and stared at each of us before continuing, "—is that Amelia is clinically depressed and the majority of her symptoms are psychosomatic."

Psychosomatic. I'd learned that word from him, too, but he wasn't the only one to throw that diagnosis around. Dr. Pierce had all but inferred that my "perceived illness"—her words, not mine—started and ended with my mind during the first and only appointment I'd ever had with her. I'd talked to my parents after my session, wondering if that's what they thought, too. Was I really going crazy? Because more and more, it was starting to feel like it. More and more, I was starting to believe it.

My dad sat me down after we got back from Dr. Pierce's office and shook his head angrily, lamenting that people have misplaced compassion. "You'll never see someone questioning an animal's suffering," he said.

Then he folded his hands over my own and looked me in the eye and opened his mouth like he wanted to say more, but he leaned forward and kissed my forehead instead.

So when Dr. Denlinger suggested I was making everything up, my dad stepped in. Again. Still, the insinuation hurt, and I didn't know what to believe.

"Do you think I'm going crazy?" I asked my mom tonight as she made herself comfortable on the bed beside me.

Because I don't know anymore. I can't tell yes from no, down from up, right from left—everything seems so backwards. I'm seventeen—the only thing I have is right now and a future to dream about, and even that is being taken away from me. I'm not graduating with my friends next year. I'm not even going to have a senior year—I may not even make it past this summer. Do you know what that's like? To be a teenager and have dreams and goals and people you want to meet and things you want to see and wonder if you'll even survive the summer? Not in a metaphorical way, but really, truly, literally.

"I believe you," my mom whispered. She leaned her head against mine and ran her fingers through my hair in long, comforting strokes. "We're going to figure this out. If we have to go to a thousand doctors, we'll figure this out."

I could hear the pain in her voice, layered with an uncertainty and helplessness that must be magnified by a thousand against what I felt for Izzy when she broke her wrist or Sam when he dropped out of school or Bilbo when he was sick and had to spend the night at my dad's vet clinic, and I imagined him lonely and scared and wondering why he couldn't be home with us, why we weren't there with him. Because if that's how I felt for my sister and my brother and my dog, I could only imagine how unbearable it must be for my mom to watch her daughter disappear and become a shell of her former self, right in front of her eyes.

The thought killed me. It killed me.

Because I love her too much. I don't want them to be hurt by this. I don't want them to see me like this any more than I want to be like this. I don't want them to be scared and feel helpless and wonder what more can they do. I don't want them to think I'm not trying to survive this—because they're the only thing that's making me not want to give up and give in.

They're the only ones keeping me from jumping.

When my mom asks me to eat the Sunday breakfast she's cooked, even though I have no appetite and no energy, I swallow a few forkfuls of scrambled eggs for her. And when Dad wants to watch a movie because that's our thing now and it's all I can do, I don't tell him the lights hurt my eyes because I want to have this moment with him. And when Izzy has an art exhibit at school, I hold her hand as we take small steps down the hallways because I'm her big sister, and I need to be there for her. And when Sammy comes over and watches me struggle to scrawl a few words down in a letter, I let him help me because he's my big brother, and he needs to feel like he's there for me.

I want Dr. Denlinger to know that. I want him to see me and my mom in my room tonight—me holding my mom's hand and telling her I love her while she rests her cheek against my head and tells me to keep fighting. I want him to see the pain this is causing and realize I wouldn't choose this. I wouldn't choose this. I'd never choose this. I want him to understand that while he's busy thinking I'm just some messed up teenager praying for attention, I have that attention, and I don't want it. I don't want my parents to be scared and hurting, and I don't want them to watch me turn into a ghost because that's what I'm becoming.

That's what happens when you survive, but you're not alive.

That's what happens when your heart keeps beating and you're barely breathing.

I'm not asking for much. I'm just asking for someone to hear me and believe me and help me save my own life.

"I feel like I'm drowning, Mom," I said. "Like I'm already submerged under water and I'm not going to make it, not like she did."

Not like the real Amelia Garrett.

My mom pressed her lips against my hair. "Be brave a little while longer for me."

"I don't know how," I whispered.

All I am anymore is afraid—not strong, not optimistic, and definitely not brave.

"Oh, sweetheart," my mom said. "There's more than one way to be brave."

We sat there in that silence together. I could feel her breath hitch, and a moment later, the pin drops of pressure as tears fell to my hair. When she finally spoke again, her voice sounded soft and faraway, like she was lost in a memory, repeating words spoken before I was even born.

"It's the battles no one else can see that you have to fight the hardest."

*It's an invisible battle…*

A memory began to stir in the back of my mind, but I was too tired to reach for it. "Did you just make that up?"

She shook her head. "Someone I knew said that a long time ago."

"Who?" I asked. "What was their name?"

"Oh, it doesn't matter."

I frowned. Names mattered—that's what she'd always taught us. They wrapped around your identity, helped shape who you were. That's what she'd always said and what we'd always believed.

"He was a friend," she finally said. There was a story in her sigh, and I leaned against her and closed my eyes. "After my mom died, your grandpa and I moved here from the city. He was the first friend I made—more than a friend, really. He lived around the corner from us, but we met at the church—at a holiday bazaar, I think it was. I'd almost forgotten that…"

*"I grew up here—over on Applewood, near the church."*

My eyes flew open, and she paused, glanced down at me, then rubbed my arm like she was trying to remind herself where she was, trying to stop herself from getting caught up in her own nostalgia.

"I guess it doesn't matter how we met," she said. I held my breath, listening to the steady rise and fall of her chest, waiting for the rest. "We called and wrote when I went away to college. When I came home for summer break, he proposed to me on top of the Ferris wheel at the high school carnival. A month later, he was drafted for Vietnam."

*"I was young. Too young."*

"I wrote him every day," she continued, "read every newspaper, watched every report wondering if I would see his name among the wounded or worse. The last letter I got from him, he asked me not to wait. He didn't think he'd be coming back."

*"The war that was…"*

"Did he come back?"

"Sometimes surviving isn't a choice."

*"The war that never should have been."*

Dark blue eyes and cigarette smoke, a memory hidden behind his smile that he never seemed to shake and I never had the nerve to ask him about. I closed my eyes, wishing I could go back a year ago and say something then, wishing I could talk to him now.

"I barely recognized him," my mom was saying, "and by then, we'd both changed. He was so despondent and withdrawn... I didn't understand why he couldn't just be happy to be alive and home with his family again. It took me a long time to understand this—there are all types of survivors, Lia."

I played with the cords on my pajama pants, rolled them between my fingers and watched them unravel again as she spoke. I remembered what she'd said to Sammy once, when he called his namesake a coward because he'd fled Philadelphia at the first sign of outbreak of Yellow Fever. Sam didn't understand how running away from tragedy could be considered anything but wrong, but my mom told him that sometimes there's more to surviving than just being alive. Samuel Breck had recorded his story for us to read and learn from, she'd said. We'd never know the horrors of those events without him.

I was too young for it to make sense to me then, but I was starting to understand it now. Some people survived and moved on with their lives, never looking back. Some people were transformed by what they endured and carried that with them forever. And some people were survivors by association—like my mom and her soldier, or Samuel Breck and his neighbors, or everyone who died last September and all of us who were left behind to grieve.

I didn't want to ask her what kind of survivor she thought I'd be. I didn't want to hear her answer—that maybe I'd be like him, wishing for the alternative and transforming into something unrecognizable, a shadow of the Lia I used to be.

*"I came back here to see if anything had changed."*

*"And had it?"*

She must have known what I was thinking because she put an arm around my shoulders and squeezed me tightly. "They bring back hope, Lia. That's who they are, even if they don't know it. They show us how to hope."

*"I'd changed. That was enough."*

For the first time in my life, I felt connected to my namesake. Because if Amelia Garrett could survive a sinking ship against all odds, then maybe I could, too.

~ *Lia*

### APRIL 11, 2002

Dear Whoever You Are,

The doorbell rang at 8:23 this morning. I opened my eyes and stared at the clock for a full minute before I realized it wasn't a dream and forced myself to sit up. I listened for my mom or dad or Izzy to answer the door, wondering in the back of my mind why I wasn't hearing shampoo bottles being dropped in the shower or the clang of dishes being loaded into the dishwasher until it registered that today was a weekday, and the silence said that everyone was already at work or school. It was just me and Bilbo and whoever had a death wish outside because the ringing turned to knocking, and the knocking wouldn't stop.

I clung to the banister for support on the way downstairs. By the time I opened the door, Bilbo was already curling himself back into a ball on the couch, and she was already walking down the driveway to her car. I called her name. She turned around and smiled brightly, practically skipping back up the sidewalk.

"You look like you should sit down," she said.

She took my arm and shooed Bilbo off the couch and told me to lie down with such authority that Bilbo and I both did what we were told. She sat on the edge of the chair across from me, her face scrunched up, and her eyes flicked from my legs to my hands to my face like she was studying me. Her hair was back to black now—no traces of the pink or purple she'd become known for around school—and it was pulled into a low ponytail over her shoulder where, every so often, she'd reach up and fiddle with the hair tie as if to make sure it was still secure.

I raised my eyebrows, but she still didn't say anything. Instead, she put her hand out for Bilbo to sniff, then scratched behind his ears while he grunted. I leaned against the arm of the couch and shook my head, trying to figure out if I was still dreaming or if this was actually real because it was getting harder and harder to figure out which was which these days.

"Are you in pain? You look like you're in pain."

"What the hell are you doing here, Mimi?"

The words spilled out of me, but I doubt I would have filtered them even if I had the energy to. Mimi Liang was sitting in my living room, head tilted to one side as she looked at me like I was some rare specimen she was evaluating in one of our science labs.

"Have the doctors figured out what's wrong with you yet?" she asked. I sighed and shook my head and sank back against the pillows. "What about your tests? They're all coming back fine?"

"All of them," I admitted.

I wanted to tell her about the knot that grew in my stomach every time I got in the car to go to another doctor appointment. I wanted to tell her how I sat in the waiting room ready to cry because I knew that as soon as Dr. Denlinger read my name on the schedule, he'd shake his head, ready to dismiss me before he even saw me. I wanted to tell her how small I felt sitting there on the exam table with another set of complaints while he read the lab reports and proclaimed they were all negative. I wanted to ask her if she thought I was a hypochondriac, too.

But I didn't. Because I couldn't bear to hear her answer.

"Tests can be wrong," she said.

I looked at her in surprise as she pulled a folded square out of her jeans pocket and handed it to me. Unfolding the piece of paper, I stared at the three-column list of symptoms, a name and phone number scribbled in pencil at the bottom of the page.

"Anything look familiar?" she asked.

Yeah. Pretty much the entire list could describe how I was feeling right then—two dozen seemingly random symptoms that my doctors were convinced had nothing to do with each other.

"My sister has Lyme Disease." Mimi nodded at the list. "Those were her symptoms."

I think I expected her to ask me how I was feeling or tell me to just suck it up and go back to school like Mollie inferred the last time I saw her. But I didn't expect that. I didn't even know what *that* was.

Mimi nodded knowingly, then stood to leave.

"Wait, that's it?" I asked. She was just going to come into my house and hand me a piece of paper and walk out the door?

She shrugged so nonchalantly, I started to get angry, and I made a move to stand, but she held out a hand to stop me. "You wouldn't believe me, anyway. People aren't wired that way. They want to think the worst, but then the worst happens and they go into denial because it can't be that easy." She paused. "The only reason my sister's alive right now is because someone handed her a piece of paper like that, and she kept searching for answers when everyone else gave up on her."

You know when they say that life is like a dream sometimes? That's how it was, seeing Mimi Liang standing in my living room, offering me a reason to keep going. I wouldn't believe it if I didn't have that piece of paper in my hands, and I doubt my mom and dad would have, either, when they came home and I told them about it.

But we gathered in Izzy's bedroom tonight and searched on her computer, digging past the statistics to read patient story after patient story that were hauntingly familiar, citing experiences so similar to mine. After an hour had passed, my dad gathered the printed pages of the research study he was reading and turned to me and my mom as we lay on Izzy's bed. He sighed and rubbed a hand across his eyes, then stared at me for a long time with a sadness I'd only ever seen once before, on a somber Tuesday evening.

"What do you think?" I asked, my words barely above a whisper.

"I think we have a phone call to make."

Five minutes. That's how long Mimi Liang was there today. That's how long it took for me to find hope again—scribbled in pencil on a folded up piece of paper.

~ *Lia*

## May 4, 2002

Dear Whoever You Are,

When I was nine, Bilbo tried to swallow a baby bird.

I'd left the front door open and was already halfway down the driveway on the way to the bus stop before I saw him bound past me, and I raced after him, arms outstretched to catch him while I yelled for Sam to hurry up and help. I thought I had him cornered against the house behind some bushes, but when I lunged for him, he broke free and pranced into the middle of the yard, wagging his tail and holding his head high. It felt like a lifetime before it registered that those weren't leaves flapping around in his mouth.

I freaked out.

My lunchbox clattered to the ground, and I started shrieking and stomping my feet, yelling at him to drop it or leave it or stay—whatever command I thought he might actually listen to, like those puppy classes he went to might actually mean something. My dad and Sam ran outside, but all I could do was point and cry and beg them to save it.

My dad stuck his hand down Bilbo's throat and pulled the bird out—a baby finch barely a few weeks old. The bird fluttered its wings and skirted under the car. I was down on my hands and knees in a second, peering at it as it pressed against the underside of the tire like that was its only form of protection. Its eyes blinked in rapid succession, its wings pressed against its back and matted down with Bilbo's saliva. It opened its beak and panted like it was calling out to its family, begging for mercy.

I cried harder.

Sam crouched down next to me. "You should have let him eat it," he said. I glared at him. "Look at it, it's suffering, Lia."

I knew that, but I couldn't let Bilbo kill it. I couldn't. Maybe it was just in shock, like that bird that ran into the patio door at the Engles' that summer. Maybe it had a broken wing and couldn't fly, and all it needed was for us to fix whatever was wrong with it so it could go back to its family and its friends and be set free again.

Maybe all it needed was a chance to survive, for someone to care enough to save it.

I begged my dad to get a shoebox and take it to his clinic because that's what he did—he saved animals. He put a hand on my shoulder as the school bus turned the corner onto our street and told me to get my books and go to school, he'd see what he could do. I picked up my lunchbox and wiped my face with the sleeve of my windbreaker.

"You're the one who made me love animals so much," I reminded him.

Then I was off, running after Sam to the bus stop, eager to tell Mollie about the bird we had rescued from Bilbo's jaws.

When I pressed Dad for details about the bird at dinner that night, he said he'd taken it to the clinic where they gave it some water and set its broken wing. They placed it on the branch of a bush outside the building, and it was gone by the time they checked on it a few minutes later.

"So it flew away?" I asked.

"It sure did," he said.

Sometimes our only choice is to believe a lie because we can't bear to accept the truth.

This afternoon, I sat with my parents in the exam room of a small, red-brick house two hundred miles away and listened to my new doctor rattle off statistics and cite studies and use words like "spirochete" and "antibodies" and "multi-systemic illness." My dad leaned against the wall, arms crossed as he listened, but every so often, he'd raise his eyebrows and grunt an "hmm-hmm…" like all this medical terminology was making sense to him. None of it was making sense to me, but I was barely paying attention. All I kept hearing were those words:

"I understand."

Dr. Howard Brennan is a small man with gray hair, a short beard, and an infectious smile. I decided I liked him immediately, even with all his degrees on his walls, and that I would continue to like him, even if he ended up being just another in a long line of doctors who patted me on the shoulder and said it was all in my head because I would believe him then.

He asked me questions about myself and let me take my time to answer, listening as I told him about how afraid I was on the Fourth of July three years ago, how I couldn't catch my breath in Mrs. Giudieri's class because there wasn't enough air in the room, how I passed out in the locker room when all I'd been doing was putting on a shoe. I told him how my body feels like it's on fire, how the confusion becomes so thick I can't remember basic words, and how I try to speak sometimes but end up stuttering, even though, internally, my mind is screaming what I'm trying to say.

If he had told me there was nothing wrong with me, I would have believed him because at least he saw me—*me*, as a whole person, and not just another set of unrelated symptoms to be recorded in a chart and filed in the back of an office somewhere.

But he didn't say I was making anything up. Instead, he listened and nodded and then, when I was done, he pointed to a single picture on the wall—a framed photograph of him, his wife, and their two sons—and said, "We were there, too. I understand."

He handed me a copy of my test results and went through the numbers line by line, explaining what he meant by an active infection.

"All this from a tick bite?" my mom asked.

"All of this from a tick bite," he confirmed.

He showed us video clips from other doctors who explained this illness wasn't rare at all, but an ignored epidemic, and handed us copies of studies from medical journals. He pulled his chair up beside me, picked up a clipboard, and drew diagrams until I understood how this bacteria had burrowed into my organs, infecting my heart and screwing up my brain and stealing days from my life.

Pieces of the conversation began to swim in my mind until I felt like I was drowning in words that sounded deceptively beautiful, like shouting profanities in a foreign language.

Borrelia. Babesia. Bartonella.

I was scared and relieved, and I didn't know which one I should feel most of all.

My head began to feel heavy, and at one point he paused and called the nurse into the room. She helped me stand and guided me back into the waiting room, where I collapsed onto an old, navy blue couch. She patted my shoulder, but not in the same mocking, metaphorical way Dr. Denlinger did. Here, she looked down at me with soft eyes and a knowing smile, and I knew she understood, too.

I closed my eyes and tucked my arm beneath my head, listening to my parents' voices filter through the thin walls as I thought about that morning when I was nine years old. I was that bird now—caught in the darkness with nowhere to go, held in a state of limbo just waiting for the world to swallow me whole. Here I was now, like that bird then, struggling to find someone to ease this suffering and fix my broken wings and offer me the slightest hope that I might be able to fly again.

Except I know you can't always fix what's broken. And like Sam had already figured out when he was thirteen and I was just beginning to see now, what we believe to be right can sometimes be wrong.

Sometimes there's more than one way to save a life.

They looked up at once as I shuffled back into the exam room. My mom looked like she wanted to reach for me, to hold me up, but she wrapped her arms around the purse in her lap instead. I turned to Dr. Brennan.

I didn't deserve any more or any less than that bird did, but there I was, huddled in the doorway and watching his eyes soften, like he knew what I was going to say even before I did, like he'd been asked this one, small request a thousand times before.

"Dr. Brennan?" My heart beat rapidly. I blinked back tears. "Will you save my life today?"

*~ Lia*

PART FOUR

Dear Whoever You Are,

I can still see it if I stand in the southwest corner of my parents' bedroom and press my cheek against the windowpane—a small section of woods wedged between Mr. Martin's wheat field and the last row of houses at the back of our neighborhood where Mollie and I used to play. I wonder if it's still standing by the time you read this, or if the builders have torn down the trees to make room for more houses to expand the development. I never pictured Mr. Martin as a sellout. Maybe he'll have his reasons.

Maybe my house is gone, too—maybe they've bulldozed the backyard and put the bushes through the wood chipper and dug up my dad's garden. Maybe all that's left of my time capsule and these letters is what's been tossed into those big, industrial trash bins before they make their way to the county incinerator. Maybe the world is just one big wasteland and nothing is left at all.

I don't care.

Some part of me cares too much.

Because as much as I hate it now, I loved those woods. They transformed the world in a matter of moments—that's it, that's all it took back then. Just a moment to climb up the dirt mound at the end of the street, loose soil turning to dust as we fought to gain our footing before passing through the undergrowth.

It was an ordinary woodland, enchanted with clusters of daffodils and layers of moss and pieces of sky peeking through the branches. We could still hear the tractors that roamed the fields behind the tree line, and the occasional honking from the highway beyond even that, but that was just background noise—part of a world that didn't belong to us anymore, one we had abandoned just as quickly as our overturned bicycles, the wheels still spinning by the time we were a hundred feet in.

We peered under fallen logs and poked at wet earth and squealed at the bugs that scurried away from the sunlight to find fresh obscurity. We picked handfuls of daffodils to place in vases on the table at dinnertime and scratched our names into tree stumps with rocks we found in the dried-out creek as if that would seal our friendship and be proof enough of our existence.

By the time we were eleven, we were too cool to collect bugs and flowers, and so we spent the afternoons hiding out in the sheet-metal fort that appeared without warning the previous spring, littered with empty beer bottles and soda cans and an old Guns N' Roses sweatshirt that might have been Sam's. We'd cleared away the debris in the fort and hung the sweatshirt as a makeshift flag—a warning to outsiders that this territory was claimed, and we'd never surrender.

But that was before. That was back when I still had some fight left in me—back when I could walk, back when I could talk, back when the woods were still this wide expanse of undiscovered thrills to a bunch of eleven year olds and not some hell that clung to the underbrush, eager to catch a ride on the unsuspecting and suck the moments out of you like an exhale steals breath from your lungs.

It's not my place anymore. I don't belong there, even though the trees still stand strong as ever. Even as I feel weaker. Sometimes I imagine they're waiting for me, wondering if I'll ever return, sorry for stealing these years of my life, and won't I give them one last chance?

Won't I?

I'm jealous of those woods. I know, it sounds stupid, right? But I am. Because they wither and decay every fall, becoming skeletons of themselves, and every spring they have another chance to thrive again and become more of what they were.

I want to be able to walk through the woods again, down a path of weeds flattened by our footsteps. I want to feel the blades of grass between my toes as I run through the meadows on my grandparents' farm in Iowa. I want to step just one foot in my own backyard without being afraid of a threat that is all but invisible.

One more spring. That's all I ask. One more chance to become more of who I am—to go to college with my friends and tumble into love and have a family of my own and grow old enough to see my kids find their place—some small corner of the world to call their own. Just one more spring …

No matter how fleeting.

~ Lia

Dear Whoever You Are,

I woke up in a cold sweat, my heartbeat keeping time with my breaths as I tried to make sense of my surroundings. There was my dollhouse in the corner, my new cell phone charging in the dark beside it. And there was Bilbo at the foot of my bed, lifting his head to check on me before settling back down to sleep. I was in my room in my house and not lost in the nightmare that still had me shaking minutes upon waking.

Dr. Brennan said this would happen—something about the die-off of the bacteria and the toxins they released amplifying every symptom so I felt worse before I got better. But I didn't think it was going to be like this. I didn't think it could get any worse.

I didn't understand what he meant until tonight.

The pain keeps getting sharper while the fatigue grows thicker, and I—I feel like I'm going crazy. I don't know what's real and what's not—everything feels unfamiliar and out of place, like the world is nothing more than a dream, but that dream becomes a nightmare—and the fact that I can't tell the difference scares me more than anything. The lines are growing more and more blurred lately. I don't know what to believe.

I wanted to squeeze my eyes shut and fall back asleep because any nightmare was better than this, but I couldn't. I lay still, trying to steady the pounding in my heart as I listened to the sounds of the house. There—that was the hum of the air-conditioning unit outside my window. And that sound there—that was only my dad snoring at the other end of the hall, a car going past the house, the shifting of the foundation. I gripped my pillow, too afraid to move.

Somebody was in the house.

No, no one was in the house. It was just me and Izzy and Mom and Dad, and I knew that. But the fear wouldn't subside, the nightmare bleeding into reality so I couldn't tell which was which. I didn't want to face whatever imaginary threat lay just beyond my door, but my parents were asleep in their beds, and Izzy was tucked into hers, and I knew I wouldn't last alone in this lingering fear until morning.

My bare feet hit the rug, and I edged my way to the door, creaking it open inches at a time until I could peek my head through. Mom had placed a nightlight in the bathroom for me at my insistence, and it cast shadows in the hallway where the light couldn't reach. My palms traced the wall as I felt my way towards the banister. I paused, listening for any sign of movement downstairs, but the only response was the drone of the refrigerator in the kitchen. I took a step, then another, pausing every few seconds to wait, to listen.

I made it as far as the living room.

The hardwood floor felt cold against my feet, and a chill ran the length of my body as I froze halfway between the front and back doors. Both doors were shut. Both doors were locked. But the dread that heightened every sense stabbed at my heart and crawled up my throat and chained me to that spot.

Something moved on the stairs. Hot tears welled in my eyes and my mind screamed in alarm, but I couldn't speak, couldn't move, couldn't warn anyone. I could only stare as Bilbo wandered downstairs, his nails tapping against the floor. He sniffed my feet and snorted before heading into the kitchen to drink from his water bowl.

I began to cry.

Upstairs, the bedroom doors opened. A second later, my mom was rushing down the stairs, Izzy right behind her. I begged them to shut every window, to check behind every closed door, to turn on every light. Izzy didn't even question me—she flipped all the light switches until the house was lit up, dispelling the shadows and easing any threats.

I think they thought I was losing it.

Maybe I am.

Mom made me drink some tea while Izzy wrapped an afghan around my shoulders, like that would protect me from the monsters that haunted my dreams. We sat like that on the couch until my tears dried and my hands stopped shaking and I grew too tired to be scared anymore. Then they helped me back upstairs to my room, Bilbo jumping on the bed like he knew he could be of some comfort now. My mom leaned down to tuck the covers around me, but Izzy stopped her.

"I got it, Mom," I heard her say.

She grabbed the nightlight from the bathroom and plugged it into an open outlet on the wall near my door, then slipped into bed beside me, resting her chin against my shoulder like she used to do all those summers ago in Iowa. When she spoke, her voice was hushed against the darkness.

"What kind of monsters?"

I leaned closer, wrapping the covers tighter around us. "The invisible kind."

I want to forget this. I want to hide away until I become more of myself again—ready to face the world and fight this invisible monster inside of me. Because I never feel safe, never feel calm. It's like I'm always gearing up for battle against this enemy that's stolen pieces of my life I won't ever get back, and I don't feel strong enough to defeat it now.

"You're going to be okay," she whispered.

I started to cry again. Not from the pain or the paranoia or the fact that I felt so weak, but because sometime in the past year, my little sister had grown up...

And I had missed it.

~ *Lia*

## June 6, 2002

Dear Whoever You Are,

I didn't know her. I'd never met her before in my life and, honestly, before three weeks ago, I didn't even know Mimi Liang had a stepsister. But the moment my mom opened the door and she introduced herself, it was like there was no before, when I didn't know her. It was like we'd always existed like this.

Briana Liang has the bluest eyes I've ever seen—an ice blue that lacks the coldness you'd expect and radiates something else. A wisdom beyond her years, my mom calls it, and because she's only twenty-two but she seems so much older, the description seems right. She has short, auburn hair that spikes in the back and sweeps in layers across her forehead, a small nose stud, and a tattoo of a treble clef and three music notes on her left wrist.

"No," my dad said when I described it to him. Just that, just "no."

I don't know—a tattoo couldn't hurt any worse than I do right now.

We went outside on the patio, Bilbo squeezing between our legs to sneak outside before I slid the door closed behind me. My neighbors had just mowed their lawn so that now it was finally beginning to smell like summer, and finches gathered on the hedge that lined our property, flitting back and forth between the branches and the rain gutters above us. Bilbo ignored them and plopped down on the cement, his head between his paws, eyes roaming over the property like he was holding dominion over the yard.

"He's my dad's dog, but he never leaves my side anymore," I told her.

"They're funny like that," she said. "It's like they can see more than people, like they know what's going on inside you."

I kicked off my slippers and crossed my legs on the lounge chair. She kept tugging at her long cardigan, pulling it closer around her thin body before picking up the belt strands and rolling the fabric between her fingers. I told her I didn't know what I would have done if Mimi hadn't come over that day. I don't know what I would have done if I hadn't met Dr. Brennan.

Now I don't know what I would have done if I hadn't met her. Because right now, I think she's the only one who really understands me.

Outside you, reading this letter, I mean.

I asked her how she knew I was sick in the first place, and she shrugged and said Mimi had mentioned what everyone was saying in school.

"What's everyone saying in school?" I asked, but she ignored me.

"It's easy to see the patterns and recognize the symptoms once you've lived with it for so long," she said. "It's real and it's scary, and anyone who says otherwise has never lived through it. You'll see."

I didn't know if I wanted to see. I just wanted to get better and put this all behind me and pretend I'd never even heard of Lyme Disease. But how likely was that? How could I even begin to ignore something that had stolen the past three years of my life like this? How could I go back to school and talk about who's dating who and what everyone's wearing and did I see the new movie that just came out when I'm barely at school. Hell, I'm lucky if I swap out my pajamas for sweatpants just to go to Sam's apartment for an hour.

I don't feel real anymore, like I'm not even human. It's like these germs have invaded my body for so long that now I'm mutated, like I'm not even Lia. I don't know who I am. I don't know who I was before this because I was just starting to figure that out, and I don't know who I'll be after this because who knows how much it has changed me already?

Am I the anxiety? Am I the loneliness and isolation? Am I the pain and fatigue? Am I the confusion—this girl who can't make sense of the world right now? Am I the auditory hallucinations that's become some kind of weird comfort because the music is beautiful and belongs to me alone, and I think, if there's anything good to come from this disease, it's that song?

Am I everything I write in these letters, wanting to belong and connect with a stranger and prove that I exist, or is even this just a byproduct of the disease—like I wouldn't have these words—or you—without it?

Dr. Brennan says these symptoms will disappear as I start to get better, but if I'm already this empty shell, what will be left of me then?

Where does this illness end, and where do I begin?

I grew quiet and stared at the lounge chair beneath me, tracing the weave in the fabric with my finger. I heard the scrape of the chair against the patio, and a second later, Briana was sitting beside me. She didn't touch me, didn't put her arm around me to comfort me—she just sat beside me. It was enough.

"Listen to yourself," she said. "No, really. Listen. Whatever speaks to your soul isn't the disease. That's just you." She reached into her pocket. "Here," she said, holding out her hand.

I stared at her. "That's a Band-Aid," I said doubtfully, then took it from her, turning it over in my hand. A dozen miniature Minnie Mouse faces stared back at me.

"I found it in my car. I don't like going to people's houses empty-handed." I raised my eyebrows, not really sure what to do with that, and she laughed. "I'm kidding. Kind of. Look at it as a metaphor. People like to make excuses for everything they do and feel, but it's all just padding—they're putting a Band-Aid on a larger problem because they don't want to admit what's really happening. Remember the Band-Aid. Remember what's real." She stood up and nudged my slippers with her feet. "Come on," she said. "You shouldn't be in the sun when you're taking these antibiotics."

Sometimes I feel like I'm all alone on an island somewhere—or, even worse, that I *am* an island. Everyone else is some other, vast continent with millions of people to keep them company, but I'm anchored here, a fixed spot on the earth, population: none.

What's worse is they're surrounded by each other and they don't even care, and you're here, your own island, trying to make up for it by caring too much. You know what happens when one person cares too much? They become submerged. They sink under the weight of their own existence, like Atlantis or Lemuria—a land mass that once thrived, disappearing into itself one plea for compassion at a time, lost to mythology because everyone's too afraid to stand up and say in more than a whisper, "I care. I'm here. You're not alone."

That's what she did—this stranger who isn't a stranger anymore.

She's one more person who has saved me from sinking.

~ *Lia*

Dear Whoever You Are,

Josh has been coming home once a week for the past month to see me. I tell him he doesn't have to, now that he has an apartment off campus and a summer job working as a line cook in the dining hall. But he says the laundry machines in his building are broken and he misses his mom's cooking and his roommate is backpacking across England—"No, seriously, just England"—so he might as well. He says that last part with a grin and a wink, and no matter how I'm feeling, I can't help but smile back.

I don't see too many people outside of my own family anymore. Briana and I call or instant message each other at least once a day to check in because she's the only one who really gets it, even though everyone else tries. I'm grateful when I can tell her how exhausted I am just to be alive and not have her freak out like my mom does because she doesn't like to hear me talk like that.

I'm surviving, Mom. If you ever read this, I'm doing the best I can—I promise. But it's hard when every day feels like a fight for your life, and every waking moment—every choice and every action, no matter how small—can make the difference between whether or not you're stuck in bed for days at a time.

I have to pick and choose now what's worth it and what isn't. I didn't use to have to make that choice.

Getting dressed is a chore, so I just don't do it anymore. Most days, it's enough to pull on Josh's college hoodie, brush my teeth, and toss my hair into a ponytail just to go downstairs and eat a substantial breakfast so I don't throw up from the antibiotics before I collapse on the couch for my morning sleep-a-thon. Sometimes my mom encourages me to run errands with her—just to get out of the house, she says, even if I have to stay in the car. So I go to the pharmacy, determined to get my own pill box to organize the medicine and vitamins that now take up half the bread drawer in the kitchen, like if I can stay in control of that, then maybe I can be in control of this.

I hold my mom's arm and shuffle across the parking lot wearing the same pair of pink pajamas I've been sleeping in all week because what does it matter? I'm a ghost now, invisible to everyone. I'm just a blur of a girl they see right through, anyway, already forgotten by the time they get in their own cars and drive away.

Surviving isn't pretty. It's hard and scary and ugly. But all I can promise is that I'm doing my best, and I'm still here.

Bethany has come over twice with brownies—not the good brownies like the kind Sam bakes me to help with the pain, making me promise not to tell Mom or Dad or give any to Izzy ever, but brownies nonetheless, and it's so nice to be remembered by her, when I feel alone and abandoned by everyone else, it makes me want to cry.

But I don't. Because crying takes too much energy, and I don't want even one ounce of what I have left to go to waste. So I sneak a bite of brownie, flipping off my doctor's orders for a restricted diet just this once, and we play board games or watch TV until I get tired and tell her thanks for being so cool. It surprises me, how cool she is, even though it probably shouldn't because I've known her for so long, and she's known me, and maybe that's why she comes over. Because she remembers I'm still the same girl, even though I feel like a stranger to myself.

And then there's Josh. Everything's different with Josh.

The guilt eats away at me most days for the toll this is taking on my parents and Sam and Izzy. I hate that I'm making them worry, hate that I can't be enough or do enough, hate that they have to be burdened with taking care of me when they've already been taking care of me my whole life. I'm going to be eighteen soon and, in less than a year, I'll be graduating high school and out on my own—at least, that was the plan, before…

But I don't feel that way around Josh—because he doesn't have to stay. He doesn't have to leave me goofy messages to wake up to or bring me green tea because he read it was good for detoxing or play video games while I sleep just so he can be with me.

"Why are you still here?" I asked him once, my voice so quiet, I wondered if he'd heard me. I held my breath, afraid that he had.

He peered at me over the top of the book he was reading before dropping it to his lap. "Do you want me to leave?" he asked, an edge in his voice.

"No," I said quickly. "But I don't want you to think you're obligated just because—"

Well… Just because.

He shook his head and picked up his book again. "Lia Lenelli, I think the Lyme has gone to your brain," he said, and it made me laugh and want to hug him because he didn't know how true that was.

I tried doing laundry for my mom, but I got confused and ended up pouring detergent on the clean clothes in the dryer by mistake. Cooking's out because I've turned on the stove instead of the oven one too many times and can't be trusted with basic kitchen appliances. And I made it all the way to the grocery store to pick up milk for my dad, but on the way back, I couldn't figure out what a stop sign meant, so I'm not allowed to drive on my own anymore. Apparently, that's what happens when this disease gets in your brain—you forget how to exist like a normal human being.

*Are you going to stay?* I want to ask my friends. Are you going to say this is too hard—there's something better out there, someone easier to care about?

Someone who's not sick?

Someone who's not me.

"Why would you say that?" Josh said when I asked him this, staring at me with eyes so wounded, I wished I hadn't said anything at all.

"Because it's true," I muttered, staring down at my hands. "I don't want to hold you back. You have this great new life at school and I—"

"You have me."

For some reason, he chooses me. Whenever I lash out because I'm so frustrated and he stays, and I cry because I'm so scared and he stays, and I'm tired and can't do much more than smile when I see him reading a graphic novel on the other end of the couch, and he stays, he reminds me of that.

He stopped by my house tonight to see if I was coming to his family's annual Fourth of July barbecue. I wanted to stay home and sleep, but I couldn't stand the thought of disappointing him. So I quickly said, actually, I was really craving one of his dad's burgers. We drove instead of walked, and I plopped myself down in a chair by the shade and watched him load his plate with food and joke with our neighbors. And I thought, at least I can do this, if only to remind him that I choose him, too.

I managed to stay outside for an hour before he had to help me upstairs to his old room, where I fell asleep as soon as I lay down. When I woke up, the sky was just beginning to grow dark, casting golden-hued shadows across the room. Through the open window, I could hear amateur fireworks going off on the far side of the neighborhood and Ginger pacing back and forth at the bottom of the stairs.

Right below the window, the voices of the Engles' guests drifted upward, like the way heat rises, each conversation melding together in a symphony. My dad was talking to Mr. Engle about all the changes at his job, now that he's a full partner at the clinic. Across the yard, I could hear Sam's laugh, and I imagined him flirting with Sarah Jacobey from down the street, now that he's single again and she's home from college. And then there was Mollie's voice, intermixed with Josh's, asking why wasn't I downstairs, and shouldn't I be better by now?

"You don't know anything." His voice was clipped with warning.

"I'm just saying… Carly says her aunt had Lyme and was better in a few weeks." She paused. "I don't think she wants to get better."

Tears burned my eyes, and I leaned back against the pillows, pressing my arm across my forehead. Is that what they all thought? Did they actually believe I wanted to be sick? Did they really think I wanted this life for myself, for my family?

Don't they get what's happening?

My mom is thinking about taking a leave of absence from teaching so she can stay home with me. And even though my dad tells her it's fine and we'll get by, it isn't fine because she loves her job, and money is what we need right now. The doctor appointments are expensive, the medicines and vitamins add up, and it's a constant fight with the insurance company, anyway, because someone, somewhere, decided that three years of illness can be cured in thirty days.

See? I'm learning this stuff. I'm reading the research studies and medical journals and patient stories, and besides that, I have enough common sense to understand that three years is a damn long time for something to do a lifetime of damage.

*Look at me!* I want to scream. Do you think I'm cured? Do you think I want this? Don't you think I want to get better, that I'm trying to push myself every single day because I want to make it to senior year so I can graduate with my class and go off to college and do something with my life?

Don't you think I'm tired of this, too?

I could still hear their voices filtering through the open window. Further out into the yard, a neighbor's laugh was deep and unrestrained, followed by a string of gentle chuckles. Tears stung the corners of my eyes but never fell. I rolled over and pressed my face into the pillow.

This was the part I hated—the reminder that life goes on.

I wonder if this is how Bilbo feels when he sits in the front hallway on summer afternoons, watching the world through a wire screen like he's imagining a time when he was young and healthy and still a part of everything, remembering what it was like to run and explore and chase what he wanted. Maybe he's still that dog on the inside, but he's not that dog on the outside—he can't run as fast, and he doesn't want to explore as much, and maybe what he wants is different, too, now that he's grown older.

So now all he can do is sit and watch and lose himself in reminiscence—so close to the world he once belonged to, separated permanently, forever, by a door neither of us can pass through.

Watching the world isn't enough. We think it should be, but it's not. Because life is still going on out there, and we're still stuck in here, wanting to be a part of it.

I took a deep breath and slid my legs off the bed, pausing to gather enough energy to stand. My grip held tight to the banister as I made my way downstairs, my legs aching and burning and begging me to stop. I leaned my head against the wall, taking deep breaths, willing the pain to pass. It never did.

"Lia?"

I opened my eyes at my name. Mrs. Engle was staring up at me, her head tilted in a way that reminded me of Mollie.

"I'm fine," I told her and reached for the banister again.

But she shook her head and climbed the few remaining stairs. "Sit down for a minute. Come on," she said, patting the carpet next to her. "Let's take your time."

The tidal wave of fatigue washed over me in a heartbeat, pulling me under and leaving me grasping for any stray bits of energy that might help keep me afloat. I lowered myself next to her and leaned against the wall.

"One step at a time," she repeated.

One step isn't enough. It's been two months, and the only thing that's changed is I'm not running into walls and falling down just from standing up anymore.

It isn't enough…

"Carly said her aunt got better in a few weeks," I said quietly. "I just want to be better already. I want my life back."

I heard her sigh, and I glanced up to see her watching me, a softness reflecting in her eyes. I could see Josh in those eyes.

"You can't rush these things, sweetheart," she said. "I know you want to." She hesitated, like she wanted to say something more, only she wasn't sure how. When she finally spoke again, there was something in the tone of her voice—familiar traces of shame and regret, like a grief that had never fully healed. "Sometimes I still think about everything I missed with my kids when I was sick." She placed an open palm on her chest. I glanced at it, then back at her, my breath catching.

"I found out I had cancer right after Justin was born," she continued. "I missed a lot of his firsts because of treatment, and it broke my heart. But I get to watch him grow up now." She wrapped her arm around my shoulders, squeezing me close. "You'll get better. You will. These things take time."

I was afraid to look at her, afraid I would start to cry again if I did. I felt bad for complaining, bad for thinking I was isolated in my suffering, like the world revolved around my pain. Because here was someone I loved who had suffered, too. And if she could get through that, what did it say about me that I was struggling to get through this?

"Oh, I know that look," Mrs. Engle said. "Don't you dare apologize for what you're feeling—not for one minute.

People like to compare their trials like one illness is worse than the other, but it's all the same. That's what I want you to understand, sweetheart. We're all just struggling to stay alive." She leaned back to look at me, her eyes glimmering under the hall light. "Just because someone doesn't understand what you're going through, it doesn't invalidate your suffering. That's just one person, Lia. You know your experiences better than anyone else. You know the courage it takes to get through this. And let me tell you one thing—hey, look at me." She reached over and took my chin in her hands. I raised my eyes to meet hers. "This is your life. You fight like hell for it."

Remember that game we used to play in elementary school when we were learning how to use computers? No, wait, of course not. I keep forgetting you're from the future where computers have taken over the world.

There was this game we played called *The Oregon Trail*. The premise was simple—you and a group of pioneers started off on a trek in a covered wagon along the Oregon Trail, and the whole point was to make it to the end without going bankrupt or losing your oxen or getting dysentery or typhoid or measles and dying. Thank God Izzy never played that game. It would have scarred her for life.

The point is, you got to choose who you wanted to be: a banker, a carpenter, a farmer... And if you died, that was it. It didn't matter how you died—one death wasn't better or worse than the other—you just did, and it was game over until you got to start again as someone new.

Sometimes I wish I could start again as someone new. Maybe I would have wanted to be prettier or smarter once, but now I just wish I was healthier. Because that's what it takes to get to the end—no matter who you are or what you're struggling with.

You just need to hold on long enough to get there.

~ *Lia*

**SEPTEMBER 22, 2002**

Dear Whoever You Are,

I didn't recognize Josh when he came to visit me today. I know I knew him—he was in my kitchen, going through the contents of the fridge to make us sandwiches while he talked to my dad. But when I came downstairs and saw him there, it took me a full five minutes to realize what he meant to me. It's those little things that make me want to cry and never stop.

Dr. Brennan is happy to see that some of my symptoms have disappeared—the dizzy spells and balance problems are gone, the tingling in my hands and feet have faded, and the music has stopped.

That last one makes me sad. Sometimes I miss the music.

Where old symptoms recede, new ones seem to be cropping up in their place. I can't read more than a page of a book at a time because I keep struggling to understand the words. I can't hold a conversation with anyone because my mind goes blank in the middle of every sentence. And I can't remember who Josh is when he's standing right in front of me.

*Josh.*

Then there's the frustration, masquerading as anger, bubbling up from somewhere deep inside of me and threatening to choke me. I want to rampage through the house, throwing books and china and tossing throw pillows everywhere because maybe seeing the destruction of something honest and good will satisfy me because that's how I feel inside—physically and mentally destroyed. It's like this disease has rewired my entire brain so I don't recognize myself anymore. I'm still me—I mean, I know it's a bad idea to break my mom's china—but it takes every ounce of self-control to keep calm when I'm screaming on the inside.

So when I went to the grocery store with my mom today—holding onto the cart for support as we wandered up and down the aisles—and an old man wearing bedroom slippers and a dark gray cardigan with holes in the elbows starting following us singing "Yankee Doodle Dandy," I wanted to whirl around and yell at him to shut up and ask why was he so crazy? I knew there was something wrong with him, just like I know there's something wrong with me. Maybe there's something wrong with all of us.

But that didn't stop me from wanting to throw a carton of eggs at him.

Dr. Brennan calls it Lyme Rage—he said it's one of the neurological effects of this disease infecting the brain and that it would pass in time with treatment with the rest of my symptoms. Briana thinks it's part of being in pain all the time, that getting angry and then blaming ourselves is a coping mechanism. I was beginning to see that firsthand. Because I feel like I'm spiraling into a darkness of what I've lost and who I've become and then, when I can't contain anymore, it begins to overflow and seep outwards, invading the space of the people who are closest, the people I love most.

"This disease isn't in your control, remember that," Briana had reassured me. "Making it your fault is the only way to find any rhyme or reason to what's going on inside of you, but it's not the answer. Your family will keep loving you even when you can't love yourself."

There was something in her voice, in the way she said that last part, that made me think she wanted the words to be true for me because maybe they weren't true for her.

She was right, of course. But just because she was right, it didn't make me feel any better.

When we got home from the store, I ran upstairs and started to write a different letter. An hour later, I heard my dad calling my name from the bottom of the stairs.

"Get dressed," he said when I poked my head out the door. "We're going for a drive."

I told him I didn't want to—that I didn't have the energy to go anywhere else—but his tone told me there was no room to argue, and I thought about how all this must be affecting them, too, if they were beginning to lose patience with me. So I grabbed my sneakers and followed him out to the car, sliding into the passenger seat beside him.

We drove in silence to the Goodwill on the far side of town, where Dad grabbed a handbasket and began loading it up with every fifty-cent piece of glassware he could find. I roamed the aisles behind him, watching him pick up milk glass vases and champagne flutes and lone dishes with hand-painted, longhaired cats staring up from the bottom of soup bowls.

My dad was clearly going out of his mind.

"Anniversary present for Mom?" I asked, holding up a ceramic clown playing a violin.

He ignored me, pulled a ten dollar bill from his wallet, and told the woman behind the counter not to bother wrapping anything.

We drove to the manufacturing plant on the other side of town—the same one where Sam works—and pulled around to the back of the building. A small loading bay was to our right, large numbers visible on the sealed doors, and in a small plot of grass beyond that sat a pile of broken wood pallets.

"Let's go," my dad said, turning off the engine. I hesitated, then followed him out of the car.

The sun was just beginning to set, but it was the end of September—there was little warmth left in the air, and I knew it would get even colder as the evening wore on. I rubbed my arms, wishing I had brought a jacket, wondering what we were doing there.

My dad silently opened the trunk, pulled out the box of glassware, and set it down in front of his car. Then he leaned against the bumper and crossed his arms. I stared at him.

"What?" I asked. He pointed to the cement wall in front of us. I glanced at it, then threw my hands up. "What? What am I supposed to do with all this?"

"Throw it," he said.

Maybe he was the one who was crazy. Maybe he was the one with the disease, not me.

"You told Dr. Brennan you get so angry, you want to run through the house and break every one of Mom's dishes."

I cringed when I heard my words thrown back at me. Tears blurred my vision, frustration beginning to simmer because it was true—that's how I felt—but that wasn't really me, that wasn't who I was. "Yeah, but I wouldn't actually do it!" I protested.

My dad's eyes softened. He nodded at the box. "Here's your chance. Have at it."

I glanced at the box, then at the wall, wondering if this was some test of self-control or something. But my dad bent down and picked up a yellow coffee mug, and I took it from him, carefully turning it over in my hands. It reminded me of the mug that used to sit on my doctor's desk—the one he sometimes reached for whenever I asked him about himself, like it was his instinct to hold onto it, to hold onto something. But then he'd catch himself and clear his throat and pick up his pen, doodling stars and suns in sweeping swirls across his notepad.

I looked up at my dad. He raised his eyebrows and nodded.

"Throw it," he said gently.

So I did.

I threw it.

With every ounce of strength I had, I hurled the glass at the cement wall where it fractured into a dozen pieces. I jumped at the sound, then turned around, a smile slowly spreading across my lips. He was right. It felt good—satisfying, even. It felt like I was shattering a part of myself I hated—this part that's so consumed by this disease it won't let me become anything else. For the past few months, I've felt like half a person, like I'm one step in this world and one step out of it. I'm a zombie dragging myself across a barren wasteland hoping for an end to this damnation, for something more than this half-life.

I think my dad knew that. I think he knew what I was struggling to understand for so long—that sometimes things fall apart so they can fit together in a different way. Maybe you have to shatter completely in order to fix the part of you that's most broken. Maybe nothing is ever really destroyed, just reshaped and glued back together with one part hope, another part faith, this part friend, that part family until we're transformed into something new and stronger and better.

One by one, glass exploded against the wall. Moment by moment, I began to put the broken pieces of myself back together. I could let myself smile. I could let myself laugh. I could let life seep back in again. It was allowed there. There, in that parking lot, I could be more than this disease.

I picked the ceramic clown out of the box and held it out to my dad. He tossed it in his hand like a baseball, like he used to do when he played softball in the fields in Iowa. It shattered into tiny shards, the air ringing with our laughter and the sound of cracking against concrete.

I stared at the pile of debris on the ground, then lifted my head to look at him. He nodded and wrapped his arms around me, squeezing tightly for just a second. Then, silently, he walked to the back of the car, opened the trunk, and handed me a broom and dustpan.

"Clean it up," he said.

Today my dad let me fall apart, then helped me sweep a thousand tears into a cardboard box to be ground and crushed and transformed into something useful.

This disease could steal my friends, my breath, my life, but it couldn't take this moment.

Not today.

~ *Lia*

Dear Whoever You Are,

There was something in her voice when she called me tonight that made me ask if she was okay. There was something in the silence of her pause before she answered that had me reaching beside the couch for my sneakers. There was something in my eyes when I asked my parents if I could borrow the car that made them say yes without hesitation.

Some things don't need to be said.

I was at Briana's house within ten minutes. She was sitting on the porch step, wrapped in a thick blanket, her head leaned back like she was soaking up the rays of the sun. Except it was night and the sky was starless, veiled by dark clouds that eclipsed even the moon. She stood when I pulled up to the curb, and I rolled down the window as she walked closer.

She asked if we could go somewhere, and I nodded and unlocked the door for her. Behind her, the subtle glow from a Christmas tree filtered past the curtains in the living room, and one of the upstairs rooms was lit up—from the street I could see the curled corners of a poster adorning one of the far walls, and I figured Mimi must be doing homework or downloading music or talking to friends online.

Briana kept the window open a crack and pressed her forehead against the glass. I could see perspiration lining her temples, but she looked pale under the passing lamplights. I turned the heat vents away from her.

"You look great," I told her. "Totally healthy."

A smile peeked out of the corners of her mouth. That was the thing—to the outside world, we probably did look healthy, except she was too thin and I was too—*not*. I bet if you saw us, you'd never guess this disease was trying to kill us both. But that's what it is. It never looks the same.

I didn't know where I was driving to, and she didn't give me any direction, so I followed a roundabout past Hastings Road and paused at the intersection to the community park.

"What are you muttering?" she asked.

"Green means go, red means stop," I said, my foot pressed firmly on the brake. When I glanced over at her, she was grinning.

That's what it's like now—post-it notes clinging to refrigerators and mirrors and cabinet doors. A daily planner checked hourly to make sure we haven't forgotten another doctor appointment. Repetitive reminders to stop on red and go on green because that's what it takes to remember even the smallest detail. Our minds have become dandelion seeds floating away on the wind, our memories scattered with the slightest touch.

"This damn disease," I said.

"This damn disease," she agreed.

The park was deserted—it was too dark for kids to play and way past the posted hours of operation. I probably would have cared about getting into trouble for trespassing once upon a time. I would have turned around and driven us to the coffee shop downtown or the twenty-four hour diner the next highway exit over, but what did it matter? I've spent my whole life being good and doing what's right, and none of it has mattered because I'm still sick. So what if I ignored the No Entry After Sundown sign? So what if we sat on the swings in the cold, her blanket wrapped around her, my nose tucked into the folds of my scarf? Being good and following the rules would have meant listening to Dr. Denlinger, and I probably wouldn't be here at all if I had, so what did it matter, anyway?

Briana clutched the metal chains and tilted her head back, inhaling deeply. "I feel like I can only breathe when it's cold."

I hate the cold. I hate the heat. I hate anything that's too much because that's all I'm becoming—heightened sensations in this illness of extremes. The cold of this winter made my body feel stiff and mechanical. The heat during the summer drained my energy and burned me from the inside out like a continuous fever. What would I do if I had to choose between one or the other? I wouldn't choose any of it. That's what I want to scream to people. I wouldn't choose a single second of any of this.

I rocked back on the swing, my feet dragging along the ground and creating a hollow in the wood chips below. If I raised my head, I could see the lights of an airplane blinking through the clouds, but that was the only reminder that there was anything above us.

I missed seeing the stars. I missed that night of Mollie's party when they felt so close, I thought I could reach out and touch them, like they were trying to reach me, too. I missed feeling like I could be one of those stars, a fixed spot in a sky where we all have our place. I missed believing I could actually be a part of something bigger like that, even though I felt so small.

I missed feeling like I belonged.

She grew quiet beside me. I glanced at her, waiting for her to say something, knowing we would enter into easy conversation in time.

Sometimes when we get together, we talk about how we're feeling or what we've learned from the latest medical studies we've read. Sometimes we'll trade ideas on new supplements to help manage our symptoms or try a new recipe packed with protein and antioxidants. Sometimes Lyme is all we talk about because this is our life now, and we have to think about how we feel and what we can eat and when just enough is still too much.

And sometimes we talk about lost stars and feeling small and afraid and permanently changed.

"I'm sick again," she said finally. Her voice was so strained, I almost didn't recognize it, even though it was just her and me, sitting there in the dark. She swallowed and bit her lip, then took a deep breath. "Dr. Brennan says it's a relapse. I know it happens—people relapse all the time. But I thought I would be different, like I could get on with my life and never have to look back."

I was silent, staring at the ground, kicking the mulch around in small circles with my sneaker. She'd left college last year because her symptoms were so bad, she couldn't attend classes, and then once she started feeling better, she pushed herself to find a job as a teller at the same credit union where Mollie's mom works. But the stress of the cost of treatment and work and struggling to get better became too much, and now she was worse—"Back to square one," she called it.

"I don't know how I'm supposed to survive this again," she said. And then her voice broke. "I don't know if I want to."

Dr. Brennan once told me I had been their sickest patient when I walked in their office that day, and I carried that around with me like a badge of honor. It was like I could finally scream it to the world, "See? Do you see how sick I was, and can you see how much better I am now?" Like that before and after mattered.

But it's not like that anymore. Because there isn't a before and an after, there's just now. And being sick isn't some badge of honor—not when you're trying to survive a disease that anyone can get and no one is paying attention. Not when everyone is ignoring the suffering that's happening right in front of them because they don't want to believe it. Not when you can spend years getting better and begin to hope you can actually survive this only to get sick again, and everything you were doing before isn't enough to heal you this time.

I couldn't argue with her because I couldn't disagree. There were times when I prayed for any release from the pain and the fatigue, no matter what it looked like. Now I didn't know which would be worse—relapsing or dying.

Because this? What we were doing, anyway? It didn't look like living.

That's what Lyme Disease does to you. It's a lonely exist-ence made lonelier by isolation, and it feels like we're just wading through life, waiting for something to end.

"Sometimes I wonder if I'm more afraid of living with this illness than I am of dying without it," I said softly. I kept my eyes focused on the ground, but I could feel her looking at me in silent sympathy.

"This damn disease," she whispered.

"This damn disease," I agreed.


Dear God,

Whoever you are.

I'm writing to you now. Maybe I've been writing to you all along.

It's been a while, hasn't it? It's been so long I don't know where to begin, and I can't help but wonder if we're strangers again.

Do you remember me?

Do you ever forget?

I've been looking for you. Yesterday, I took my mom's car and went for a drive. Don't worry—it wasn't very far. Just to the church at the end of the neighborhood where a few empty cars were parked, scattered across the lot. I sat in the front seat and stared up at the stained glass window, at the cross on top of the steeple, and I tried to find you. I tried to find you, but you weren't there.

Today, despite the cold that burned my lungs and the icicles hanging from the gutters, I stood on the patio and stared up at the gray sky and snow filtering through the bare branches of trees that won't sprout buds for another four months. I tried to find you there—tried to feel you somewhere along the wind—but the sky was just sky and the air was just air, and the snow fell to the ground like that was where it always belonged.

I thought I could find you in the stars—so bright there's still a part of me that believes I can touch them, like that winter night when the universe felt so big, and I felt so small, and I thought illusions could be conquered. But that was a lifetime ago, when constellations were more than a cluster of stars and wishes belonged to burning streaks of light. Even if you are there, hidden among the Milky Way, you're still light years away.

I don't know how to pray, and I don't know how you'll hear me if I can't say the words. But I'm writing you this letter because it's the only voice I have left, and he told me once that there's a power in words, even in a whisper.

We're billions of voices on this planet struggling to be heard, trying stand up and say, "Here I am. I exist. I am here and I am now and I have something to say. I matter because I'm alive, and I have my own story to tell."

And you... You see us and you hear us and you force us to be more of who we are through the stories we live, removing the mask with each photograph or brushstroke or word written on a lined piece of paper and tossed into an old lunchbox. That's what everyone is doing, when they paint enchanted scenes on canvas and carve wood-grown tulips and write words on a page. It's another way for us to be heard, stripping us down to just our voices, speaking in the only way we know how.

But sometimes words aren't enough.

You know what happens if you keep a caterpillar in its chrysalis? It dies. It suffocates trying to become something else—the one thing it's meant to be. When it can't change and grow and transform, it shrivels up and becomes nothing instead.

That's how I feel right now. I feel like I'm dying—I'm struggling to exist and be something else when this disease is suffocating me, keeping me trapped in a life that was meant for more.

I want to talk to you. I want you to hear me.

I want to tell you how I keep searching for you when I look to the stars and how I desperately want to imagine they're billions of little beacons lighting up the darkness and guiding me to who I'm meant to be, once I break free from this cocoon.

I want you to remind me that today will pass into tomorrow and the day after that and the day after that, and I'm never so lost that I can't be found.

I want to find you, but whenever I catch a glimpse of you, I can't ever reach you.

And so I've just stopped trying…

Waiting, instead, for you to find me.

*~ Lia*

PART FIVE

Dear Whoever You Are,

I don't know you. I don't know who you are or where you are or when you are—I don't even know if you're still reading this or if my time capsule is still buried and forgotten the way some dreams—even the waking ones—should be. That's okay. Maybe I shouldn't be writing to you in the first place. Maybe I shouldn't be saying anything at all. It's just that these letters are a type of communion for me. I'm in pain when I'm awake and I'm frightened in my dreams, but I'm safe here in these words to you, when I might otherwise suffocate from all the unspoken thoughts and become less of who I am...

When I already feel like a fraction of who I was.

Maybe I'll never get to travel and see the world, but if I have all these pieces of myself out there—if these letters are scattered in a million different places—maybe it will prove I was here, that I was a part of it all.

Maybe someone will remember me.

I sat outside on the front step this morning, Bilbo beside me, watching Mrs. Woodward prune her hydrangeas across the street. Dr. Brennan had warned me about being outside while I was on my medication—something about skin sensitivity—but I didn't care. I know I'm not invincible, I know I don't belong to anything more than this moment, but that made me feel even more reckless and bold and strong.

Let the sun try to burn me now.

A sedan ambled down the street, slowing at each mailbox. Bilbo lifted his head and followed it with his eyes, a low growl making its way past his throat. I rested a hand on the back of his neck and watched as the car pulled to the side of the road. Mrs. Woodward looked up, her pruning shears paused mid-cut. The car door slammed shut, and I tried my best to hide a smile as he crossed the street and up the driveway.

I hadn't seen him in over a year, but he looked exactly the same—and also different. It was his eyes… They were lighter than I'd ever seen them, like they were no longer holding onto something he wanted to forget.

"What are you doing here?" I asked.

My doctor smiled. "I'm selling my place—moving up to New York permanently."

"To be with your girls."

He ducked his head in a nod. "And my wife," he said, his smile growing wider. I couldn't help but smile back. He paused and stared up at the house, like he was seeing it for the first time, even though he'd grown up only the next block over. I wonder if things look different when you've been away for so long. "Is your mom home?"

"At the pharmacy."

"Oh." He paused. "You look—"

"Like I haven't showered in a week?" I tugged my base-ball cap further down on my head. "'Cause that's a truth."

His mouth twisted upwards in a hard-fought grin. "I was gonna say like hell, but that works."

I laughed. The sound was foreign to me, like a language I'd never heard, and I wondered how long it had been since I last laughed.

"Can I?" He motioned to the step, and I nodded and scooted over, pulling Bilbo closer to me to make room. He sat down, scratched the scruff on the back of Bilbo's neck a few times, then folded his arms across his knees. "Your parents called me."

My head shot up. "Both of them?"

He glanced at me, confusion shading his eyes. "Yeah, of course. They thought maybe it would be good if you had someone to talk to about all of this."

I grew silent and stared down at my hands. "Josh calls me every night. He talks to my mom or dad or Izzy when I'm too tired, but he always calls to ask how I'm feeling."

"He's still at school?"

I nodded. "It makes me feel good, to know that he thinks of me, that I haven't been—" I stopped myself, took a deep breath and looked up at the sky, at the clouds that eclipsed the sun. "He says Mollie asks about me, but I don't know if he's lying just to protect his sister or to make me feel better, or if he's actually telling the truth."

"Which one matters more?"

I shrugged. I'd told my parents I didn't have the energy to care, but I do. I do care. I care because she was my best friend, and when times are bad, that's when you need your best friend the most.

But she's about to graduate and go off to college to start her future, while I'm still here trying to figure out if I even have a future. Dr. Brennan says I do. Just by being in treatment and taking care of myself means I'm on my way to getting better and someday, I'll be able to do all the things I've always wanted to do. But it's hard to imagine having a life when you're feeling worse than ever. And it's hard when the rest of your friends are going about their lives and yours is put on permanent hiatus, like a bad TV show hanging in the balance between renewal and cancellation.

I watch a lot of TV these days. I've also started to write more.

"Mrs. Giudieri sent me a book of creative writing prompts," I told him. "I'm working through them one at a time—drafting short stories and emailing them for her to read."

"Speaking the words…" He nodded and smiled. "Good, I'm glad."

"They're not always there, though—the words."

They come and go like an ocean tide, pulling away before I can reach them, leaving only traces of what I wanted to say behind.

"They'll come," he said. "Give it time—keep writing—and they'll come."

We sat in silence for a while, knowing there was so much to say and not knowing how to say it. Across the street, Mrs. Woodward had abandoned her hydrangeas and moved onto a bed of newly-bloomed daffodils, and nearby in the yard, a butterfly landed on a blade of grass, then fluttered across the lawn and out of sight. Bilbo heaved a sigh beside us and nuzzled his face between his paws. I reached over and ran my fingers along his back.

"Do you think Josh will ever forget me like Mollie has?" I asked.

"She hasn't forgotten you," he said. "No one forgets anyone—they just change and grow apart, learn to love each other in a different way."

"Like you and my mom?"

I felt his eyes on me, studying me, wondering what I knew. He wasn't surprised—at least, if he was, he didn't show it.

He glanced down at his hands, then lifted his gaze across the yard. "I'm sorry. I should have said something right from the beginning—to both of you."

"I don't care about that," I said quickly, and I didn't. It didn't matter—I'd realized that a long time ago. Because that was my mom's before and what I cared about was what came after. I stared at my lap, at the holes in my jeans, and picked at one of the loose threads at the knees. It began to unravel, and I bunched it back up and tucked it beneath the fabric. "She told me that when you came back—you know, after the war—that you were changed." I looked up at him. "Is that going to happen to me?"

He whipped his head around, pain etched across his face. "God, no. Lia—no. Not like that," he said. "God, not like that." He sighed and ran a hand along his jawline as he fought for the words. "I wish I could say something that would make this easier on you. What you're going through—it's a different kind of hell. Yeah, it's going to change you, but everything changes you." His eyes searched mine, desperate to find some recognition there, some reassurance that what he was saying was understood. "You're more than this."

A car drove past, and we both watched it for a moment, soaking in his words.

I had a cat named Tempest once. My dad brought him home from the clinic after he came in as a stray and no one claimed him. He was so gray, he was almost black, and he reminded me of the storm clouds in Iowa—the way the sky can change in an instant. He used to scoop water from his bowl and drink from his paw, and he slept on a corner of my pillow at night, purring until I woke up long enough to reach above my head and scratch behind his neck.

Flashes of memory, that's all they are. I don't remember the touch of his head nuzzling my hand, or the strands of fur like velvet through my fingers, or how he'd jump in my lap when I was sick with a summertime flu, like he knew I needed that comfort. I don't remember what it felt like to hold him.

"Is that what it's like?" I said quietly. "Is that what it's going to be like with me, when I'm gone? I'll become memories and scarcely even that? Because that's my answer."

His eyes narrowed as he watched me, blue eyes clouding over to match an Iowa sky. "Your answer to what?"

"Your question—the one you asked me that first day we met in your office, when I told you about my time capsule. I need you to ask me again."

He knew that was coming. I think it was the real reason he was here. He nodded slowly and turned his gaze across the lawn. "Okay," he said. "What are you afraid of?"

My dad found my lunchbox this morning. I could hear him holler for my mom from the open window in my room, then he came in the house and called up the stairs and held up his hands—the statue of the turtle lying flat in one palm, my lunchbox resting in the other. He said he'd found it when he was planting the Knock Out rosebush and asked me what it was doing in his garden. I love that name. Knock Out Rose. It's like it belongs to a great female boxer or something.

A fighter. A warrior.

I could tell my dad was half-confused and half-amused by his smile, but when I told him it was my time capsule and opened it up to show him my letters, the smile faltered and he paused, like he didn't know what to say.

Four years of letters buried in a pink, plastic My Little Pony lunchbox two feet beneath the soil in the backyard garden. Four years of tears and anger and loss and heartache under the vigil of a ceramic statue. Four years of stories to prove to the world who I am and what I loved and that I existed.

That's what I was afraid of. That none of it would matter.

My doctor tilted his head and looked at me, a familiar frown creasing his face. "That's not all you're afraid of, is it?"

No. But it was close.

I told him to hold on a second and went into the house to grab the lunchbox from where it waited on the kitchen table. When I sat back down on the front step and opened it up, he looked inside—at the dozens and dozens of letters creased and folded and bound by a rubber band—

And didn't say anything.

I felt stupid. I thought he might say it was stupid. In a way, it kind of is. But he gently pushed it back in my hands and closed the lid until it locked.

"Keep writing," he said. "One day, when you're ready to move on from this, you'll want to write one last letter. But I don't think you're finished yet. Keep writing."

I don't know if anyone will find this, but that's not why I'm writing now. Even if it's only me coming back here from wherever I am to dig up this time capsule and read through these letters, that will be enough. Because I want to remember this hell I fought through.

I want to know what I survived.

~ *Lia*

**MAY 24, 2003**

Dear Whoever You Are,

I saw Mollie today. It's the first time I've seen her since Thanksgiving, now that I'm not in school anymore. She came into the bookstore where I work, the bell above the door jingling in a way that always makes me smile. It's a ghost of a sound—light and airy and barely noticeable if you aren't expecting it. That's how I feel these days—like you'd barely notice me if you weren't paying attention, and every time I hear that bell, it's like a reminder that we're both still here.

Briana got me this job at her aunt and uncle's used bookstore a month ago. It used to be an old general store that was converted into a deli in the sixties, but when Briana's aunt and uncle bought the building, they refurbished the wood floors, painted the shelves a light gray, and turned the deli cases into book displays. Now I spend two hours a day cataloging donations and researching prices before heading to the upstairs apartment to check in on Briana.

She left home soon after she relapsed because her parents didn't believe she could be that sick again. Except she's not that sick again. She's worse. Her parents told her she would need to get a job if she wanted to start taking antibiotics through an IV—like that was a choice, like anyone wants to shove a PICC line in their arm and get pumped full of medicine on a daily basis. Like anyone chooses this life to begin with. But they didn't want to hear that, and she didn't know how to make them understand.

When her aunt and uncle found out what happened, they sold their house to help her pay for treatment and moved into the empty apartment above their store. Briana moved in with them, and now she works at the front desk on the good days, and I help cover for her on the bad.

Her mom came into the store once, asking for her. She looked at me for such a long time, I thought maybe I was having one of my memory lapses or had somehow failed to hear her question.

"You have it, too?" she asked with such an air of familiarity, I wondered if Briana or Mimi had mentioned me.

I nodded. "I wouldn't be here without either of them."

I didn't mean "here" as in the shop, even though I owed them for that, too. I meant *here*. The literal here. Because maybe if Mrs. Liang heard how both of her daughters had helped save my life, she could see how much Briana needed her mom to help save hers.

But Mrs. Liang only stared at me, studying me the way Mimi did when she sat in my living room last year. For a moment, I thought there might be a glimpse of compassion there. For a moment, I thought she might be starting to understand just how serious this illness really was. But then she glanced around the bookstore, adjusted the strap of her purse along her shoulder, and said I didn't have to tell Briana she'd been there.

I went home an hour later and hugged my mom and dad.

"What's that for?" my mom asked.

"Nothing," I said.

Everything.

I was sitting behind the counter this afternoon, digging through a box of books, when the bell above the door rang. My heart sank when I glanced up and saw Mollie walk in. She looked around like Mrs. Liang did, like she was seeing the store for the first time, even though it's been here in the middle of downtown for the past six years.

I didn't want her there. I know how that sounds, but this bookstore has become another world to me, my home away from home. This is a place where I can feel safe and relaxed, a place where I can finally escape myself and this illness and have some kind of purpose. Seeing her walk through the door, I couldn't help but be disappointed because she was my life out there, not my life in here.

She kept her distance. Her eyes skimmed the titles on the shelves, even though I knew she wasn't really interested in the books, and she fiddled with the straps on her bag, winding them around her fingers before letting go and starting over again. She was nervous. We'd been best friends for over ten years, and I'd never seen her this nervous before—not even when we called Scott Abernathy to invite him to her tenth birthday party.

Her gaze flicked to the books and papers spread across the counter before landing briefly on me. I waited. I didn't want to be the first to say anything—I didn't know what to say, anyway.

"So, you're working here now?" she asked. "You're not going back to school? Ever?"

I could see the judgment in her eyes, even if she didn't mean for it to be there. It was the question I'm sure a lot of people were asking—the question Mrs. Giudieri asked when I told her I was getting my GED instead of waiting until I was better to go back to school and graduate.

"Are you sure you're ready to make that decision?" Mrs. G. had asked.

Translation: Are you sure you're ready to give up on school?

But I wasn't giving up. That's the thing people didn't understand. I tried attending school part-time, but I'd never know if it would be a good day—a good hour, a good minute. Some days, I'd be fine for the first two periods and then crash during third. Other days, I'd feel better in the afternoon, but then my energy would drain by dinner. I couldn't depend on time anymore. I never knew, minute to minute, how much I had left.

My mom took a leave of absence from her work at the college so we could do home support, but I was sleeping eighteen hours a day and couldn't even keep up with that. Everything I had worked so hard for was gone. It slipped through my fingers faster than I could blink, and it was going to take everything I had just to build my life back up again.

Getting my GED meant I could start to do that. I could work in the bookstore for as much or as little as I needed to. I could take a course at the college here or there. I could start believing I had tomorrow just like everyone else. Someday, I'll be able to dream again about traveling the world and going away to college to become a researcher or a doctor or a writer or whatever I want to be—whatever is more than this—but right now, this was what I could do.

"So, what are you gonna do next year?" Mollie asked. "You're really not going to college?"

"It's kind of hard to look that far ahead," I said. I could see her visibly flinch, and I remembered having this same conversation with Sam when he admitted he was dropping out of school.

*You don't get it,* he'd said, his voice soft and pained. And I didn't back then—back then, I thought changing your mind meant giving up, that deciding on a different future meant throwing your whole life away.

I didn't understand that sometimes it's okay to choose another beginning.

I was being hypocritical now, and I felt bad, but I didn't want to admit it. I didn't want to be the first to say I was sorry here.

Mollie sighed. "I didn't know," she said, but her tone was so casual and half-hearted, I could only stare at her, any sympathy I'd felt for her vanishing completely.

What did she mean she didn't know? I spent all of twenty minutes at the dinner table at Thanksgiving before retreating to Josh's room to sleep because I was so tired and in so much pain, I couldn't sit up anymore. She was the one who took me to the nurse when I passed out in gym class last year. She was there when I freaked out about the fireworks and then again when the world felt lost and faraway at her birthday party. She's been there since the beginning.

"That's the thing, Mollie, you did know," I said. "I'm sorry if you were too busy making out with Benji Harris to realize your best friend was dying."

Yep. I regretted those words. Maybe not the words themselves because they were the truth, but the way I said them. Briana had told me a long time ago that there wasn't any room for blame in our lives, that although I could be angry at Dr. Denlinger for being so dismissive and Mollie for being so absent, it wasn't entirely their fault.

"People only know what they've been taught," she'd said. We were sitting on the floor of my room, tracing patterns in one of Izzy's sketchbooks and shading in the empty spaces with colored pencils like I used to do in my doctor's office all those years ago. "Until they want to learn, we can't teach them anything."

The words echoed in the back of my mind now.

"It's fine, I'm getting better," I told Mollie. I glanced down at the pencil in my hand, tapping it against my leg. I hated the fact that even now, I had to comfort her, when I was the one who had spent the past year scared and lonely and hurting. "It's just—I didn't think I would. And some days are bad and some days are good, and some days it feels like I'm still dying, and I just really needed someone. I really needed my best friend."

"You had Josh," she said. "You were always spending time together, and then you just ditched me at my sleepover and then again at my birthday party—"

That was ages ago. A lifetime ago. How was she bringing that up now after everything, when I had apologized over and over for walking out of her birthday party, when now she knew the truth about what happened that night. And how could she blame me for spending time with her brother when he was the only one there for me outside of my family, when he became my best friend because my best friend couldn't even bother to call?

I tossed the pencil down on the counter. I was defeated and tired of fighting. My whole life is a fight now—I'm fighting every single day to beat this thing, just to survive, and it takes its toll, beats you down. And it's not just one fight you either win or lose—it's been a constant battle every minute of every hour of every day for nearly a year.

Maybe all those people who were afraid of Y2K and the asteroid were onto something when they hid out in their bunkers, seeking shelter when the world threatened to end. Maybe they were just too tired to stand up and fight anymore.

I was tired. I didn't want to fight anymore.

And I didn't want to fight anymore with her.

"Josh wasn't you," I said.

I shrugged—that would be the end of it. I didn't know what else to say. I told her I was happy for her—that her mom had shown me pictures of her and Benji at prom, that she looked beautiful, that I was sure she would be successful at school. We'd see each other in July and again at Thanksgiving, but we didn't have to pretend anymore—not when the thread between us wasn't just broken, but lost completely, and nothing else was binding us together.

She was in tears. I wished I could cry, too, but I didn't have anything left in me. She swiped at her eyes with the back of her hand, then reached into her purse. "I asked Carly if I could have her extra ticket for you," she said. "I know you don't want anything to do with school any-more—and you probably don't want to go—but no matter what you think, you're my family, and I want you there."

She placed the ticket on the counter. I stared at it in silence, "Graduating Class of 2003" glaring back at me in large block letters.

When we were little, we used to play dress-up in her basement, imagining we were going to balls and dances and our senior prom. We rode our bikes in circles in an empty parking lot and dreamed up lives for our future selves—attending the same college, sharing an apartment in a charming, anonymous city, working at an art gallery or a hospital or a zoo. We giggled excitedly in Josh's car on our first day of high school, already planning our senior year spring break to somewhere exotic like Brazil or Australia or California and then backpacking across Europe or Asia or the Midwest once we graduated.

We were so stupid.

We were so young and innocent and beautifully stupid to think our stories could be linear like that, without plot twists and endings, always traveling parallel to each other.

"It's not gonna be the same without you," she said.

The bell above the door jingled as it closed behind her. I slid the ticket across the counter, looking at what could have been my future in a different time, another place. It's what I wished I could make her understand—that stories change and lines converge and separate, and strangers become friends and friends become strangers—

And the world keeps spinning, anyway.

~ *Lia*

## June 7, 2003

Dear Whoever You Are,

Graduation day. I suppose you're expecting me to say something about how I wish that was me up there in the white robe, smiling while Colby Donahue gives a speech about leaving high school to embark on our greatest adventure yet, thinking about the future and leaving this town behind to go wherever it is everyone plans to go to do whatever it is they plan on doing.

I bet you think I'm ready to cry and reach into my bag for the tissue I stuffed in there along with the commencement program that lists all my friends' names as the graduating class of 2003. You probably think I scanned that list, mentally calculating where my name would be if I were sitting on the football field with them—right there between David Lacey and Ally Lennox.

I know you're expecting me to wonder what if... What if that was me, crossing the stage and shaking hands with the principal and moving the tassel on my cap to the left or the right—or whichever way announces that you're an adult and ready to face the world on your own.

But the truth is, I'm not. Because those what ifs disappeared a long time ago, and that Lia who imagined her graduation day is filed away in the could have been, but isn't now. It's buried beneath another life, a different outcome, a separate story.

Down the row, Mr. Engle cups his hands over his mouth and hollers while out across the field, Mollie smiles on stage and shakes the principal's hand, dipping her head to show off the top of her graduation cap she's decked out in rhinestones. I can hear Mrs. Engle's gentle clap, followed by an audible sigh, and then Josh's deep chuckle and Justin's "Yeah, Mollie!" beside me. I can't bear to look at any of them because when I do, I see the pride beaming through their smiles, and that's what gets me.

I'm glad my mom and dad aren't here right now—glad that for them, today is just another day. Dad has appointments scheduled at the clinic, and Mom had to go into the office to prepare for her summer class, now that she's teaching at the new college. And I'm relieved because I can't bear to imagine how they wanted that to be me walking across the stage, diploma in hand.

I wish I could have given that to them.

I wasn't kidding when I told you I watched my life slip through my fingers. The thing is, even though I'm getting better—even though I'm worlds apart from where I was this time last year—this illness is going to shadow me for the rest of my life. Not just because there's always the possibility I can relapse once I'm better, or the fact that I can just as easily get infected again.

When I renew my license and can't check the organ donor box, I'll be reminded of just how badly these germs have invaded my entire body. When the church at the edge of my neighborhood or the pharmacy out on Hastings Road hold their annual blood drives, I'll have to keep driving past, knowing I'll never be able to save a life that way.

I'll have to spend the rest of my life explaining to employers how I got my GED instead of graduating with a diploma, and I can't tell people why because they wouldn't understand. I'll be a lie holding onto my truth—that this disease damages you in the eyes of the world, and even though you piece yourself together and build yourself back up, you never know when things might fall apart again.

Things fall apart. It's just what happens. And each time they do, you have to find the strength to put it all back together again.

*~ Lia*

Dear Amelia,

Do you remember the litter I delivered a few weeks ago? Six blue nose pit bulls, all healthy. Their owner brought them in this morning to be checked out. The runt reminds me of you. She was the first to open her eyes, and she's small, but I can tell she's going to be feisty.

When you were born and your mom told me she wanted to name you after some passenger aboard the Titanic, I thought she was crazy.

(Don't tell your mom that.)

Sam was fine. My great uncle was Samuel, and it's a good name. At least I could pretend we were naming him after family. I never understood your mother's obsession with names and human tragedies. We have enough hardship in our lives, I didn't see why we should want to remember any more.

I think I see it now, thanks to you, Lia.

I want you to understand something. We try as parents to do what's best for our kids. We love them and provide for them and try to be what they need us to be. We can help heal a broken heart. We can fix a bruised knee. We can hold your hand when you cross the street, when you fall down, or when you're afraid.

But we can't save you from yourself.

Through your name, the real Amelia Garrett gave you something we couldn't—proof that you were meant to be here, on this earth, and with us. I think she survived to show you that you can, too. Your mom probably already knew this, smart woman that she is.

(Do me a favor? Don't tell her that, either.)

I fear I've failed you as a parent and as a medical professional. I see animals come into my office with Lyme Disease every year, and I should have caught it. I'm sorry. You're my little girl, and from the moment you opened your eyes, I vowed to protect you. I'll never stop, I swear it.

I'm not so good at this. I just thought I would add something to your time capsule on your graduation day. I want you to know how proud of you I am.

Love,
Dad


AUGUST 3, 2003


Dear Whoever You Are,

We went for a drive today—past the fields that grow wheat in June and corn in August and down the back country roads that can get you lost forever, if you try hard enough. The windows were open a crack—just enough to let the warm summer breeze whip my hair into disarray, but I liked it that way. I felt free here with him. More free than I'd felt in months.

My sunglasses created an orange film over the dandelion-painted grass and faded farmhouses as we crested a hill. Out of the corner of my eye, I could see Josh pause from watching the road and glance over at me. I didn't say anything. He reached over and rested an open palm on top of my head, shaking me gently.

"Get outta there," he teased, his smile wide. "You're thinking too much."

If only he knew. It's all I can do these days—think and dream and wish for another chance at this, a different life. But this is all I know right now, and my only escape from what's really happening is to write my wishes in a letter and hope that when I sleep, it will be a good dream and not the lingering nightmares that now come in waves.

Sometimes I wonder if I'm really meant for this life. I mean, this disease is trying to kill me, anyway, and I'm only a year above legal. I still can't buy alcohol or rent a car, and I've never been anywhere but Iowa, and that doesn't really count.

I want it to count.

All of it—I want all of it to really count. I want my life to matter. But how can it matter when my life hasn't even had the chance to start?

I don't know why I wrote that. I don't really mean that. Of course my life matters. It's just… I want more than this. I want more than days sleeping on the couch because I can't make it upstairs to my room. I want more than a few hours at the bookstore, more than one class at the college. I want more than text messages from friends making empty promises to come by and see me this summer before they leave for college or to backpack across Asia or to start their jobs at the corporate center near Hastings Road.

I want more than one Sunday afternoon drive along winding roads with Josh.

His hand fell away from my head, his fingers lingering, tangled in the strands of my hair, before pulling away completely. He glanced at the road, then back at me, his eyes darkening with concern at whatever he saw in my own.

"Lia?"

I forced a smile. It was all I knew how to do. "I'm okay."

The tracks of his CD player changed—a somber song that matched the mood. Neither of us made a move to change it. I turned to look out the window, barns and groves of trees passing too quickly and not fast enough all at the same time. The car slowed, and Josh turned down a gravel path lined with clusters of wildflowers that were so out of place, they could only have been scattered there by the wind. I folded my sunglasses and tucked them in the cup holder.

"Just hold on..." he said, a smile in his voice.

We pulled past a run-down farmhouse in need of fresh paint, an abandoned bicycle lying on its side in the front yard and fresh linens hanging on the line out back. Horses grazed in an open field as we drove alongside a split-rail fence. My hands began to shake, and I gripped the door handle and stared at the tall grass and the woods that lined the far end of the field, knowing the threat that might lie in wait in the overgrowth.

"I don't want to be here, Josh," I whispered.

He reached over and tucked my hand inside his own. "Look at me," he said, rolling the car to a stop. He brought his hand up to cup my cheek. "I won't ever let anything happen to you."

We turned left—away from the horses and the field—and rounded another corner. Soon, the dense outline of trees opened up to a dirt path, which gave way to sparse plots of grass layered by railroad tracks. Pieces of old railroad ties were rotted and broken, some sections of metal completely overgrown with moss so that the line disappeared entirely before reappearing again and continuing on as far as we could see. A single platform sat to our left, a set of crumbling cement stairs the only way up. White columns that once held a roof now supported nothing—a canopy of branches created by the nearby maple trees blocked out the sun so that only small flickers of light filtered through the overhang. In front of the platform sat half a dozen train cars, still resting on the rails as if suspended in time—or sixty years too late.

Beside me, Josh put the car in park and paused. "We don't have to—"

"I want to."

I wanted to more than anything, despite the vines that threaded their way through the windows of the passenger cars and the meadow grass that grew wild alongside raw metal.

I wanted to walk among the abandoned—the lonely and forgotten—and imagine a time when the vibration of the trains moved the floorboards beneath the platform as metal tore against the tracks and whistles echoed for miles, harmonizing with conductors who bellowed arrivals and departures. I wanted to stand vigil in this graveyard, where reunions and goodbyes took place in the same heartbeat, before the last ticket was sold and the train came to a permanent rest.

I wanted to exist beside these empty relics that mimicked the landscape of my own desolate heart because here, in this deserted space, I was my own wasteland.

I stepped out of the car, my shoes crunching over the dirt that would soon turn soft under the bends in the grass, and hesitated. A few feet ahead of me, Josh stopped and reached back for my hand. It felt warm and safe, and I thought, he could lead me anywhere, and I would follow him.

I asked him how he found this place, my voice barely above a whisper. I didn't want to disturb the sanctity of this place. I couldn't.

"I came to see you that September. After...you know. Sam had called me—said you weren't doing so well, so I came home and wanted to come by, but..." He shrugged. "The world felt so messed up then. And we'd only just said goodbye, and I didn't think I could do it again. So I went for a drive and took a wrong turn and ended up here." He paused. "I guess I figured if the earth could take back what was hers, maybe you could, too."

There it was. That way he says things the way no one else does. The moments like this where I wonder if I'm still dreaming because those dreams feel more real than life sometimes.

He dropped my hand and turned his back to me, bending his legs low to the ground. "Here," he said. "Jump on."

I blinked. "You're gonna carry me?"

"Yeah." He shrugged. "So you don't have to walk through this stuff. C'mon."

So I did. I wrapped my arms around his neck and leaned my body against his back. He tucked his arms beneath my knees and stood, scooping me up with him. He turned his head and asked me if I was okay. I nodded and burrowed my face into his neck, wrapping my arms tighter around him and pressing my lips against his skin.

"Thank you," I whispered against his shoulder. I felt his smile more than I saw it.

We walked through the growth and over the railroad tracks, pointing at the empty windows and graffiti art that had been painted—now faded—on the sides of the trains. We peeked inside the carriage cars, laughing at the layer of dust that kicked up when he dumped me on one of the faded seat cushions, and squeezed through the openings in the boxcars, where light broke through punctures in the metal like stars on a cloudless night. Our shoes scuffed the dirt on the floors as we pushed against doors that had been rusted shut with time. With a groan, the metal gave way, and we grinned stupidly at each other and sat on the edge of the boxcar, our legs dangling over the sides. His fingers interlaced with mine as we watched the sun dip behind the tree line, washing the platform columns in a flood of golden light.

I wish I could take a picture of that moment, because when you can't trust memory, sometimes a picture is worth a thousand times more. I wish for a million more moments like it.

I want that chance.

"I don't want to forget this," I said quietly. "Do you think I'll forget this?"

He turned, confusion briefly sweeping across his face as his eyes locked on my own. He let go of my hand and reached up to cup my cheek, his thumb running across my skin with a tenderness I'd only ever known from him.

"Never."

I hope that by the time you read this, I'm old and gray and sitting somewhere next to Josh. I hope I have pictures of us dancing in the rain or walking along the shore of some sandy beach, or whatever it is you're supposed to do when you're an adult and in love like this.

Because sometimes words aren't enough. And these letters to you—whoever you are—don't feel like enough. And maybe pictures and memories aren't even enough, but memories are all you have, when you want to remember moments like this.

*~ Lia*

EPILOGUE

Dear Friend,

Sometimes I walk downstairs in the mornings and still expect to see my mom packing my lunch for school, wedging a ham and cheese sandwich between the thermos and a banana, sneaking in a handwritten note on a napkin when she thinks I'm not looking.

Sometimes I think I'll see my dad watching the baseball game on mute late at night, an admonishment ready to pass his lips when he sees I'm up past my bedtime, his eyes softening when I wordlessly curl up on the couch beside him and tuck myself beneath his arm.

Sometimes I imagine Isabella drawing sweeping lines across the sidewalk in pastel chalk and Sam rinsing off his Camry with the garden hose in the driveway, the soap suds catching the sunlight long enough to create an iridescent mosaic before dissolving altogether. Sometimes I move a little to the left when I walk through the kitchen doorway, still expecting Bilbo to brush past me in his eagerness to be fed.

But the Camry's gone now. So is Bilbo. And we're all so much older, those moments becoming lost, distant memories that make me catch my breath when I stumble upon them. Sometimes they seem so close at hand, it's hard to remember it's been years and years since Mom scrawled my name on a brown paper bag—years longer since she closed the lid on that My Little Pony lunchbox that's waiting to be buried one last time beneath a garden statue whose paint has faded from so many summers under the sun.

Those scenes feel so real sometimes—like living, breathing memories. And when I realize what they are—that they're nothing more than forgotten moments, tucked away in the folds of who we were—I can't help but feel sad that this is all we become: moments and memories and scattered stories.

This pain has become a memory, too, more distant than the day before, but it never goes away. Memories are like scars, reminding me how I fought this illness—fought for my life—but that's just one battle while the war still lingers dormant within me.

I know what Briana meant then, when we sat on the swings in the cold all those months ago. It's the only thing I'm afraid of now, a whisper in the back of my mind, wondering what if I relapse or, worse, get infected again with a different strain, another illness?

I don't think I can battle through hell a second time.

I don't think I can survive that again.

The last time I saw Dr. Brennan, there was a discharge notice paper-clipped to the front of my medical chart—a plain, manila folder that had grown thick with three years' worth of test results and symptom scales marking my improvement. We'd stared at each other in silence, both of us knowing that our lives had already been irrevocably changed once and how quickly it could change again. He'd smiled then, the lines around his eyes deepening, a promise engraved in his words.

"I'm not going anywhere."

Some days, I still don't think I'm past it, like I just can't let it go. In some weird, twisted way, I don't know if I want to. It's like I'm clinging to the memory as some form of protection against the world because I still don't know who I am without this disease. It's changed me into someone better, stronger, and I don't want to lose that again, this person I'm becoming.

"Revise the story," Mrs. Giudieri told me once. We met every month or so this past year at the coffee shop down the block from the bookstore. She helped me submit a couple of short stories to some local writing contests and, every so often, she'd review a new piece I'd written and hand it back to me, half of it crossed out. "It's weighing it down. You don't need it."

I would gape at the paper in my hands. It was like my freshman year of high school all over again—the day Mrs. Hadley gave me my first "D" on a test. Staring at the writing she'd just annihilated made me want to cry because all that time and all those thoughts and all these words were worthless now—nothing more than wasted effort.

But she just smiled knowingly. "It doesn't belong in your story anymore. But that doesn't mean it never did."

I know she's right. I've lived that part of my story, but it doesn't belong here anymore. Now, it's just a link between the past and my future—like these bare walls and the wooden dollhouse that's still sitting in the corner of my empty room as I write this.

This is my last letter.

Tomorrow, Josh will help me pack the car with the remaining boxes of clothes and books and kitchen supplies that's now piled near the front door, and we'll drive upstate to meet Mollie in our apartment, where she'll help me hang Izzy's paintings on the walls of my room and point out the best shortcuts across campus. Mom and Dad will hug me a thousand times as I tell them it's getting late and I have to go, but halfway down the driveway, I'll tell Josh to stop the car, and I'll jump out and hug them again, whispering I love you over and over and over, if only once out loud. Sam will call twice while we're on the road—once to wish me luck and again because Briana wants to make sure I got her gift—a pack of Band-Aids I've already tucked in a box next to a bouquet of wooden tulips.

Those goodbyes are saved for tomorrow, when I close this chapter of my life with a faint memory of who I was and look forward to who I finally have the chance to be, knowing my story isn't ending here.

Tonight, I'm writing my goodbye to you.

Dozens of letters to you, and I still don't know who you are. I don't know your name or where you live or how old you are or who you love. I don't know anything about you. But I don't have to for you to mean something to me. You know me—better than anybody. You let me cry and get angry and be afraid and fall apart. You let me put myself back together again, hour by hour, letter by letter.

Because of these letters, I'll exist long after I'm gone. Because of you, someone will remember me. They'll know who I was and that I lived...

And how we all survived.

~ *Amelia Garrett Lenelli*

# AFTERWORD

Dear Reader,

How do I begin to express what writing this book and having you read it has meant to me? I feel like I've already said it all, pouring my thoughts and fears and very own experiences onto those pages, and yet there's still so much more I want to say...

This book, while primarily a work of fiction, is grounded in my own experiences of living with late-stage, Chronic Lyme Disease—including the struggle to find a diagnosis, the complications that come with treating such a complex illness, and the emotional toll that years of fighting for your own health can take on the soul.

In early 2012, I was diagnosed with Lyme Disease and multiple co-infections, which further complicate the disease, after over fifteen years of inexplicable illness and constant misdiagnosis. Through the years, I'd been handed various diagnoses as reasons for the fatigue that consistently plagued me and the myriad of seemingly unrelated symptoms that followed, one by one. I'd learned to manage the limitations as best I could, tucking each diagnosis in my back pocket as I pursued dreams and strived to live a full life.

It wasn't until having surgery to remove an infected gallbladder in the fall of 2011 that I found myself in a sudden, rapid state of decline that worsened over a period of six months. I was at my doctor's office every other week, in the ER half a dozen times, visiting specialist after specialist as new symptoms began to crop up even while others failed to abate.

In the meantime, I struggled to work: my signature on documents became nothing more than an illegible scrawl while blocks of text were incomprehensible, like reading a foreign language. I struggled in my own home: I leaned on walls for support because I couldn't maintain my balance, shuffling from room to room because I was too weak to lift my feet and sleeping on the couch because I couldn't climb the stairs.

Fainting due to syncope, neuropathy in my hands and feet, electric shocks running through my neck and shoulders, air hunger, heart palpitations, derealization and anxiety, and, worst of all, unbearable fatigue… These were Lia's symptoms because they were my symptoms—just as they are the same, shared experience of hundreds of thousands of people who are fighting this disease.

It's hard for me to write about it even now. But I didn't think I would survive then. Test after test came back negative, and doctor after doctor presented me with yet another diagnosis until they started to stack up the way kids collect baseball cards: Chronic Fatigue Syndrome, Fibromyalgia, PCOS, Migraines, Depression, Anxiety, Vitamin Deficiencies, Hypotension, Peripheral Neuropathy. I couldn't understand how my body could be breaking down like this, when I was barely into my late twenties and continuing to get worse. I couldn't accept that these were all separate issues and not a result of one root problem that was causing my body to go haywire.

It didn't make sense.

I kept trying to put the pieces together, scouring online medical journals and patient testimonies on message boards for stories that were similar to my own, for something that would point me in the right direction and help me save my own life, even as my health continued to decline.

*Trust yourself,* the voice inside kept nudging me forward as I began to question myself. *Keep searching, keep fighting. Don't give up yet.*

But I wanted to give up. Because even when I found the answer that seemed to connect all the dots—even explaining symptoms I'd had for years that I didn't recognized as symptoms (tinnitus, easily crying, obsessive-compulsive tendencies, persistent weight gain)—it still wasn't enough.

My research kept leading me to the same conclusion: Lyme Disease. I naively thought it was simple enough— now that I had a name, I could get treatment and get better. But when I broached the subject with my doctors, they insisted that my previous tests had all been negative and refused to pursue the possibility further.

I cried. It was really all I knew how to do anymore. I felt alone and abandoned, and I didn't know where to turn next. I remember calling my mom on the phone, crying to her from my place on the couch after my neurologist refused to give me one of the more sensitive Lyme tests.

"I give up," I sobbed in defeat. "I don't want to fight anymore."

"Then I'll fight for you," she said.

The next morning, I received an email from someone who had seen my plea on a message board. They'd provided me with the names and numbers of local Lyme

Literate Medical Doctors (known within the community as LLMDs). After speaking to the nurse for an hour and a half, I hung up the phone and shed new tears—tears of hope, tears of relief. It was a start.

I'd heard of Lyme Disease in passing when I was younger—adults were always warning us to pull our socks up when we were playing in the woods (not the fashion statement you want to make when you're an adolescent), and I knew a distant family member had been diagnosed with it years ago. But those were idle warnings—so far removed from our daily existence that they were easy to ignore.

I didn't know then how dangerous Lyme Disease could be. I didn't know how easy it was to become infected—that ticks carrying Lyme have been found in every state within the continental United States, or that the disease could be congenital or sexually transmitted, as recent studies suggest. I didn't know how it could damage the body and steal moments from a life. I didn't know that finding a diagnosis was only a small battle amid a misrepresented, often political war.

And I didn't know that treatment could be so complicated—that getting better meant first getting worse due to the Jarisch-Herxheimer reaction—or that healing would become a promise you make to keep fighting for your life again and again, every minute of every hour of every day.

Lyme Disease is a multi-systemic illness, made infinitely more complex by the presence of co-infections. It's caused by the *Borrelia burgdorferi* (Bb) bacteria, which invades the body's joints and organs while impacting the neurological and central nervous systems. Lyme Disease is known as

The Great Imitator for its ability to mimic everything from Chronic Fatigue Syndrome, Fibromayalgia, and Lupus to Multiple Sclerosis, Alzheimer's, and Parkinson's Disease, leading to misdiagnoses and underreporting even while reaching epidemic proportions. It is currently the fastest growing vector-borne illness in the United States with over 300,000 new cases per year—a staggering figure that still fails to account for the number of patients who receive false-negatives on testing that is notably inaccurate. Without a proper diagnosis, which is too often the case due to inaccurate testing and willful medical ignorance, the bacteria, known as a spirochete for its corkscrew or spiraled shape, can destroy the body and mind, allowing patients to slip through the cracks, crippled by a disease that society denies and a system that refuses to save them.

I began documenting my journey with Lyme Disease on my personal blog years before I even knew I was sick. Writing has always been my catharsis, and having that outlet when I began treatment not only allowed me to express those heavy emotions, but it connected me with others affected by this illness—both patients themselves and supportive loved ones. The loneliness and isolation that this disease fosters breaks you down. The knowledge that you're not alone is what keeps you going.

Sharing our stories and our struggles has been the greatest source of comfort and inspiration when facing an illness that makes it difficult to find either. While I'm still in treatment four years and one relapse later, I'm also worlds apart from where I was at the beginning of this health journey. I didn't realize then what a war this could be, how many battles would have to be fought, or just how many lessons there were to learn. I didn't know what it meant to be a survivor. I didn't know what it meant to be brave.

But I know that sigh of relief when you realize you're not alone. I know what it means to fight for your life and for your future, to hold onto the promise of something better, to look forward to a healthy tomorrow.

*The Last Letter* is the story of my own struggle with Lyme Disease, shrouded in fiction to create a separation from my own experiences that became necessary for my own catharsis. Although I'd spent years detailing my life on my blog without restraint, I was afraid to get too close and relive the pain, the isolation, the depression, and the fear of losing my sense of self—and my life—all over again.

But I wanted to share my story, knowing that my experiences with Lyme Disease and similar chronic, "invisible" illnesses are shared by hundreds of thousands of people across this country and the world. I *needed* to write this story, knowing that the number of Lyme-specific cases keeps growing exponentially, knowing that there are so many others, like me, who feel alone in their suffering and are struggling to just be heard.

I had something to say, but I didn't know how to say it. I had a story to tell, but I didn't know how to tell it.

Until Lia offered her voice and the right words followed.

Living with an illness as complex as Lyme Disease is a challenge physically… Actually, I'm understating that. To be perfectly honest, the physical symptoms are often a hell itself. But it also takes its toll emotionally, and that's specifically what I wanted to bring to light in this book.

Because it's isolating and lonely, especially at times when you feel like you're only existing in the world instead of living in it. It's frightening and frustrating, especially when you feel like you've been abandoned by a medical community that chooses to deny your suffering and a society that refuses to recognize your pain. It's filled with a sense of loss for your old life, a guilt for how it's altered the lives of those you love, and a regret that you can't be everything you once were—everything you wanted to be—especially when it feels like this disease is all that you are.

This disease is not all that you are.

This disease is not all that you are.

This disease is not all that you are.

*You are more than this disease.*

It took me a long, long time to separate myself from this illness, from this pain. It took me a long time to realize there could be blessings here, too. Because while this disease is full of loneliness and frustration and loss, it's also full of community and hope and rebirth. Lyme lives here, but so does faith and courage and strength. This disease changes you, yes, but it also shows you compassion and kindness; it helps you find the courage to stand up for others, for what matters. It makes you brave.

So thank you to the doctors, friends, family, and caregivers for standing with us. We know it's not easy, but we need you. And we love you. You might get tired of hearing it, but we'll never get tired of saying it—we're so grateful for you.

And to those who are fighting Lyme Disease, similar illnesses, or your own internal battles: I know the bad days feel like hell. Hell, the good days kind of feel like that, too. But those bad days also show you what you're capable of—they help you shout to the world, "Hey! Look what I've been through, and I'm still here." They help you reach out to those who are struggling themselves and remind you that you're not alone. And they prove that you have more courage within you than you could ever imagine.

So stay a little longer. Fight a little harder. And know that I'm always fighting with you.

*With love,*
*Susan*

# MORE ON LYME DISEASE

Lyme Disease is a complex illness in its manifestation, diagnosis, and treatment; however, for the sake of this book's focus on the emotional impact of living with such an illness, certain aspects were simplified to allow for a basic understanding of what patients experience.

To learn more about the nature of this disease, please visit the following resources:
*(Note: The author of this book is unaffiliated with the following organizations.)*

### GLOBAL LYME ALLIANCE
### (www.globallymealliance.org)
Global Lyme Alliance is the leading private non-profit organization specializing in the prevention, diagnosis, and treatment of Lyme and other tick-borne diseases through science-based research and education. Renowned for its grants program, which funds world-class research aimed at providing measurable advances in Lyme Disease treatment, Global Lyme Alliance also offers innovative education and awareness programs for the general public and physicians, including a new comprehensive educational curriculum for students.

## INTERNATIONAL LYME AND ASSOCIATED DISEASES SOCIETY
## (www.ilads.org)

In a sea of medical organizations laying claim to understanding the diagnosis and treatment of Lyme Disease, ILADS is one of the foremost non-profit medical societies that takes into account the severity of the disease, the urgency for education and long-term care, and the research demonstrating the persistence of the Borrelia burgdorferi bacteria in Chronic Lyme Disease patients. ILADS provides updates to Lyme Disease and co-infection research and legislation as well as information regarding diagnosis, treatment, and recovery for both the patient and medical community. The ILADS website also includes physician referrals in conjunction with their ILADEF (International Lyme and Associated Diseases Educational Foundation) physician training program.

## LYMEDISEASE.ORG
## (www.lymedisease.org)

A prominent Lyme advocacy organization in the United States since 1989, LymeDisease.org provides news, information, and analysis via an extensive educational website, email newsletters, blogs, social media, and its esteemed online journal, *The Lyme Times*. It also sponsors MyLymeData, a patient-powered research project that focuses on Chronic Lyme Disease. Additionally, LymeDisease.org offers a network of online support groups while working with Lyme advocates throughout the country on both local and national legislative and awareness efforts.

## UNDER OUR SKIN: THE UNTOLD STORY OF LYME DISEASE
### (www.underourskin.com)

An award-winning documentary from Open Eye Pictures, *Under Our Skin: The Untold Story of Lyme Disease* brings to light the hidden epidemic that is Lyme Disease, as well as the political controversy surrounding its diagnosis and treatment. Its recently-released sequel, *Under Our Skin 2: Emergence*, continues to investigate the obstacles that researchers, physicians, and patients face, even while the epidemic expands to a global scale. Both films provide an invaluable resource to patients, physicians, and caregivers in understanding the complicated nature of Lyme Disease and why its diagnosis and treatment is infinitely more complex.

## NATIONAL SUICIDE PREVENTION LIFELINE
### (www.suicidepreventionlifeline.org)

Patients with Lyme Disease and other tick-borne infections are at risk of suicide due to the documented psychological manifestations of Lyme and accompanying decrease in quality of life. If you or someone you love is suffering from depression and/or suicidal ideation, please contact your physician immediately or call the National Suicide Prevention Lifeline (1-800-273-TALK).

**To learn more about the author's personal experiences with Lyme Disease, please visit:**

**Author Website:** www.susanpogorzelski.com
**Facebook:** www.facebook.com/lostinthelymelight

SUSAN POGORZELSKI

35159902R00167

Made in the USA
Middletown, DE
22 September 2016